MW00912482

Small Rain

Small Rain

John Harris

New Star Books
Vancouver
1989

Copyright © 1989 by John Harris

All rights reserved. No part of this work may be reproduced
or used in any form or by any means – graphic, electronic, or
mechanical – without the prior written permission of the
publisher. Any request for photocopying or other reprographic
copying must be sent in writing to the Canadian Reprography
Collective, 379 Adelaide Street West, Suite M1, Toronto,
Ontario, M5V 1S5

Some of these stories have appeared previously: "Making Light of
the Love in the Moon" in *Writing*; "Making the World Safe" in
New Directions; "Local Initiatives" in *Capilano Review*.

Canadian Cataloguing in Publication Data

Harris, John, 1943-
  Small rain

ISBN 0-919573-94-0 (bound). – ISBN 0-919573-93-2 (pbk.)

I. Title
PS8565.A77S6 1989   C813'.54   C89-091400-1
PR9199.3.H37S6 1989

The publisher is grateful for assistance provided by the Canada
Council and by the Cultural Services Branch, Province of British
Columbia

Printed and bound in Canada
First printing September 1989
1   2   3   4   5   93   92   91   90   89

New Star Books Ltd.
2504 York Avenue
Vancouver, B.C.
CANADA V6K 1E3

Contents

Westron wind, when will thou blow?
The small rain down can raine.
Christ, that my love were in my arms,
And I in my bed again.

Making Light
of the Love in the Moon.

My ex-wife lives upstairs in the bedroom with en suite plumbing. When she dresses for work in the morning I hear her water go down the drain. My children sleep in various rooms around the house. They are budding musicians and when they aren't on their instruments or piano or drums they play their tape decks. My girlfriend lives across town. When I am with her I am happy again, and when I am away from her I am anxious. I bathe regularly after work to dissolve the bunched knot in my shoulders. I lie awake for hours at night. I worry. I cry, sometimes, softly, a vague mist in my eyes, and all over nothing.

Once a month, I consult my psychiatrist. This has been going on for two years. Three times in the course of a seventeen-year marriage, I snuck into other women's beds. And I mean snuck. I felt the appropriate guilt and love. When she kicked me out I lived in agony. When she took me back we screwed like rabbits. Then, at her request, I built a room downstairs and slept there. I figured something was up. When she told me about her friend and we separated I felt ambivalent. I was glad it was over. I wished her luck. I dreamed about her body. Then I met my girlfriend and the dream went out like a blown candle.

Presently, however, I am impotent. I keep a list of reasons

in my wallet. In consultation with my psychiatrist, I revise the list. My guilt over my ex-wife is rapidly moving down. My desire to live with my girlfriend is rapidly moving up. My psychiatrist keeps trying to push it down. He says I am insecure. I have been pushed out of one nest and only want into another. I have known my girlfriend for only a short while and already I want to live with her, to marry her. That is why I sweat in her bed. That is why I am numb from the waist down. It is better to be self-confident. It is better to be free. That is the source of potency.

I guess I'm not the confident type. I need somebody. When my girlfriend asked me for a date, I couldn't believe my luck. I was nervous. I felt like phoning my mother. I bought a corsage. I almost got beat up in the bar. I was watching the door too closely. The guy sitting beside the door gave me the finger. I asked what was bothering him. He said I was staring at him. I said if I was going to stare at someone it sure as hell wouldn't be him. This was temper more than courage. The guy was young and big. If it came to a fight I would probably have my glasses wrapped around my face or shoved down my throat. I was lucky. His friend held him back.

When she came into the bar looking for me her eyes were large in the dark. She kissed me. I felt like jumping for joy. She sat down and took her coat off. She asked me if I had herpes or anything. She said maybe we should sleep together, get it over with. She said she had to send her little boy to Vancouver to visit his father. Would he give him back? She wanted to get a custody order because they never did get married. She asked me how you do that but I didn't know. We walked over to another bar where a friend of mine sat down and talked to us. He is into politics. She sat smiling at me while he told us his concerns. When the bar closed, we walked to the park. Two weeks before, a woman was raped and killed there, in the willows along the river. The mist was waist high. We stopped by the indian graveyard and kissed. The moon came up and filled the sky. "Just like it's supposed to," she said.

A few weeks later, when I lay helpless on her, she said

nothing, but slid down beneath me, took me between her fingers and slipped me into her mouth and I came finally over and over into her and then she held me very hard until morning. After two years of stumbling through the bush. After two years alone in a basement room, waiting for something to happen, doing my job, watching TV with the kids, going to bed at ten o'clock. I knew I was there.

Two weeks later, I went to my doctor. I thought, if this interferes between me and her, I'll slit my fucking throat. I wanted to make a commitment. I wasn't going to take it lying down. I went up to his office. I told him my concerns. He looked at me gravely. He is a religious man, and every five years he does voluntary work in India. There are pictures of him in the local paper with sick Indian kids. "What do you expect?" he said. "You're getting used to somebody new. You're anxious. It'll take awhile. Anxiety pushes your blood pressure up, makes it harder to perform. We never recommend intercourse for heart patients, for example, unless it is with a spouse or long-term partner. In that case, it is highly recommended. Otherwise, the risk is very high. You'd be amazed at how many middle-aged men die in the arms of prostitutes or casual lovers."

I started getting an erection. He told me how erections can be artificially maintained if the base of the shaft is manually constricted so the blood is trapped in the penis. He told me to change my habits of arousal. "You've probably been masturbating too fast," he said, "perhaps in a state of self-disgust. Slow down. If the erection dies, wait it out. Limit your fantasies to your girlfriend. If you really love her, then she's the one you want." I thought, how wise he is. Maybe it's memorized out of a textbook. If so, how wise we are. If only I could die in her arms, in the distant future of course.

My friend Harvey tells me it will be very hard to wake up again. There will be a lot of emotional ups and downs. "Get used to it," he says. "It's good for you." He is just up from Nanaimo, to work in the bush for a few weeks. His logging boots are pinching his feet. He shaved his head on a dare just before he left Nanaimo and now he regrets it, wears a fedora everywhere. He scared himself in the mirror. He thinks he must be close to the edge. Who would shave his head? he wonders. What's happening in there? Besides, it's colder up here than it is in Nanaimo. He asks me about my girlfriend. I tell him we are taking up skiing. "New love, new life," he says.

As I understand it, in every relationship you get to a point where you live together. She says we can just do our jobs and (hopefully) fuck but there are times when her eyes are lonely and times when I cry alone and times when our kids drive us crazy and times when the bills are too high and one or both of our vehicles is or are broken down. Still, we are afraid of too much intimacy. She says it's a matter of body chemistry. Sometimes it can be forestalled by having separate bedrooms. Once bodies are in contact they will adjust and become very similar. Once that happens, she says, it is game over for the relationship.

Right now, there's not much chance of that happening. I live in the basement like a skunk. My kids patrol the house with loaded Sanyos. My ex-wife is upstairs with her own friends. My bed is narrow. I do have a fireplace. The Italian I bought the place from loved cement. The house looks like a gun battery but there are fireplaces in the basement and living room. I write poems and stories but I don't know if that's a plus. I have a steady job but it bores me. I have no money. I have to send the kids to university. I have grey hair at the temples and wear the sweaters my mother sends me and the socks and shirts I get from the kids for Christmas and birthday presents.

My girlfriend has a nice suite and a little boy and dozens of old friends who love her maybe as much as I do. I meet them and wonder where they have been all my life. She has taste. It is built into her. Everything she wears is beautiful. An old friend built the bed that she sleeps in. She likes to dance but doesn't drink much. She craves a smoke and one cigarette makes her sick. She craves a coffee and can't drink it all. Sometimes she eats a deluxe mushroom burger with chips and feels sick for an hour. She likes to sit and neck in the car with our pants pulled down to our knees and the police cars patrolling up and down the boulevard. We stay there for hours. Her eyes shine. "What comfort," she says.

She goes regularly to group therapy. There is a great anger in her and she doesn't know why. It seems obvious to me. It is the big question. People are selfish and sicken in their pride while love and innocence go begging through the world. Even if people are mad from boredom or disappointment they should have grace. They should try not to harass other people or infect them with cynicism. When she is put down by her social worker she swears. When her lawyer is drunk she hangs up on him. When the neighbours are cruel to their children she goes and hammers on their doors and yells at them. When her friends freak out on drugs or get drunk or mean she breaks phones and dishes on the floor and smashes the glass tops of coffee tables.

She tells me about this when we are in bed together. Sometimes we are at her place and her kid is asleep in the next room. Sometimes we are at my place and the stairs are busy and the fridge door opens and closes until the early hours of the morning. She says, "Fuck, this is bizarre." But we kiss and hold one another and come separately into one another's mouth and hands and when I awaken later the light from the fire is flickering on the ceiling and she is breathing easily and her face is smooth as lake water.

She is a lucky lady. Her little boy is happy. One day I took him to the park. My girlfriend had to get some work done. He was shy with me and sucked his thumb and rubbed his eyes. But he liked the swings. I pushed him on the swings and the airplane. I pushed him up and down on the teeter-totter. I followed him up the steps of the slide and then caught him at the bottom. He heard a sound and said "train?" so we walked down to the river to watch it go by. He said "carry" so I picked him up and he put his arm around my neck and by the time we got back to the car he was almost asleep on my shoulder, one hand in his mouth and the other tangled in my hair.

I think I will fall in love with him soon too. Then how deep in will I be. How fast to get there and how far to fall. But I've fallen before. Maybe my girlfriend will get tired of me or I'll get tired of her. What defeats us is the repetition, says the poet. Maybe I've acquired a taste for it. I've acquired a taste for children. I follow mine around now that they are older and come home only to eat and maybe sleep. I go to the after-school soccer game to watch them take on the fuckfaces from the school across town and when the game is over they wave at me from across the field and pile into cars and go off to celebrate or commiserate and I go home. I attend concerts where they perform on flute, clarinet or trumpet and when it is over I go out the side doors and wonder why I never listened to that music before.

She asks me if I really need to start that all over again. "Christ," she says. "Sometimes I feel so hassled, like the little bugger is eating me alive." She points out that I've never been alone. I left my parents and married and had kids and now my kids are almost gone and I'm grey and carrying a little boy through the park. How do I know I don't want to be alone when I've never tried it? I imagine myself driving home from work to a bachelor apartment, reading Tolstoy for a project, carrying a corsage to a new girl every spring, writing letters to my children and visiting them for a week in the summer. What would I learn?

My psychiatrist thinks I should be alone. He wants me to get out right now. He thinks that's part of my problem. He thinks I am doing more harm than good by staying at home. "What about your girlfriend?" he says. "How could she go there?" "It must be hard on the kids," he says. He says they need to see the break, the change, otherwise it is like everything is going on as before and maybe those feelings are as before but they aren't or are they? "Do you still love your ex-wife? Of course you do but then she is going down her own road and your concern and care are out of place there. Even if it is convenient to live in the same house it may not be the best thing. Maybe you should be alone for a while."

It will be hard to leave my kids. Maybe they will have to

leave me. That's their right. Besides, real estate is down and houses aren't selling and it takes both of us just to make payments. The kids think it's weird alright, but they all say so what? My girlfriend can come over any time. They will stay out of the basement. Maybe they will babysit the kid. I tell them that I will have to get my own place. When winter is over I will move out. Maybe I will go back to the farm where we used to live and fix the place up and their old rooms will be waiting whenever they want to come out and I will come around as usual to take them out for supper and drive them places.

It's not that easy. There is fear in their eyes that I will slip away too soon, too fast, into my girlfriend's life or some other girlfriend's life and I will be sitting in some other kitchen with a redheaded little boy on my lap, feeding him as I fed them. There is fear in me for them and their lives and my ex-wife and my girlfriend and her baby boy when they are out there away from me, the killers lurking in the willows. I'm not a man. I don't know where to go. I'm frightened. For me, sitting in the bar waiting for my girl. For the girls who show their legs and the boys with shirts unbuttoned who desire them. For the children who do their best to do what we say. For the men and women awake in their beds or out on the street. For everyone looking for love, crying over nothing, jumping for joy.

Are You Alright?

When Donna walked into the classroom we thought, something is going to happen. Wilma was enough, "real nice," Barry said, but we knew she had registered for herself and a friend. We were two guys, on the prowl. We waited, but Rod had already started in on the responsibilities of the first-aider, and was giving us some absorbing descriptions of his experiences as an ambulance attendant. We forgot that the chair beside Wilma was empty.

Then the door at the side opened and Donna stepped in. Long legs in new jeans. High heels, fur jacket, thick hair. She rummaged through her shoulder bag and produced her text-book. Then she looked up, blushed, and strode to the empty chair beside Wilma.

Rod had stopped in the middle of an accident scene where a policeman (great guys but notoriously weak in the stomach) had fainted while gripping the brachial vein of an accident victim to prevent blood from pumping out of a severed wrist. The whole class was watching Donna.

Barry and I glanced at one another. This was it. Two guys and two girls. The rest of the people in the class faded into caricature. There was an old guy and a fat kid. There was a student nurse, filling in one of the requirements for her college program. There was Greg, a young guy with a shy smile who wanted to be a para-med. There were a couple of middle-aged women. It was Donna and Wilma, John and Barry.

We were cool. Actually, we were almost dead. I was living by myself, learning how to get up, shave, and go to work with the knowledge that my ex-wife and kids were on the other side of town. I had a girlfriend, or had had one, with whom I was in love, had fallen instantly in love when she asked me out, which was as soon as she heard from Barry that I'd signed the papers. I lost the girlfriend, sort of. She kept coming around. After seventeen years of marriage, what did I know? Barry was married with two small kids. He'd just been given notice of termination from the college where we work together. The charge was redundancy. They were going to use computers to teach English. There were excited guys in three-piece suits who came up with the computers. They were very young. They talked about goals and objectives, outcomes and dacums. "Dacum and I want to go home," sang Barry. He was depressed one day, high the next, so I proposed the first-aid course. It got us out on Wednesday nights. We felt we were doing something practical about the doom that was gathering around our lives. We were learning how to cope with real disasters. We were gaining a marketable skill.

So Donna and Wilma were a problem and a promise. Our hands were tied. We could socialize. We could have some laughs. That's what we came for. We could see how it went. We went for three weeks, sat beside them, some jokes moving back and forth. Then one night after class when we were parking the Rescuci-Annies downstairs Barry said, "I told Wilma you're a doctor. I think they're interested. Ask them out."

So we went to the bar that night. Wilma went home early. Donna stayed. We told her everything. She told us everything. She told us she'd never met a guy she could actually imagine living with. She told us she'd like to have a kid. She told us how she hated the fuckers who ran the finance company where she worked, the whizz-boys in the manager's office or from out of town who kicked you down and then offered to

pick you up, who screwed up your life and invited you to cocktail parties in their homes or hotel rooms so they could screw
you too. She imitated their approaches. She said she was 29.
She was one angry, funny lady.

We went out regularly after that, after every class, shutting
the bar down. The first problem we had to sort out was the old
guy. When the class split up into groups of three (one for pulse
and vital signs, one victim, one attendant) the old guy and the
fat kid were left out. The fat kid was hard to bandage. You
couldn't get a splint between his legs. The old guy had
wandering hands. After the first practise session, one of the
older ladies quietly announced that she wasn't going near him
again. He talked too much and too close to your face. He wore
a couple of layers of long underwear and two pair of socks. He
didn't have a pulse. Barry and I arranged to take him if
Donna and Wilma bought us a drink after class. They got the
fat kid.

On Sunday afternoons we went to Wilma's place to practise
splinting. Then to Donna's. Then to Barry's, where Joy laid
on coffee and cake and gave us some pointers from a course
she'd taken a few years before. Then to my place. First time
I'd ever known any working girls. They live like gypsies, get
kicked from town to town, have to listen to the banal
confessions of married men over and over again, in kitchen
corners at cocktail parties, with the wife glancing over from
across the room, at home at night over the phone, sometimes
in broad daylight during working hours. Getting paid shit and
going nowhere and no way out but to actually hook up with
someone and hope he turned out to be human and not much
sign it was a fair probability. They were angry. It curled my
toenails which were already getting ridged and yellow like the
old guy's. "You guys," said Donna one night at the bar, "You
are the only people I've met in three years in this town that I
can talk to."

"Fuck," said Barry later. "I don't think Wilma is too interested in us, but Donna is. Did you notice we don't have to ask
her to come to the bar. She just does. She likes you, John."

"I think she likes you."

"She hates married men who fool around."

"That's me alright."

"That was you. You're a changed man. Look at the practical side; you're the available one."

"I asked her to dance last Wednesday and she said no."

"I asked her the week before that and she said no."

"This time we'll both ask her."

You couldn't have found a pair of less desperate cases. I was thinking this was my chance to cut out, go off by myself, work on a novel or something. But I knew what I'd really do if I ended up staring at the top of a desk for a year. I'd start dreaming about Donna or my ex-girlfriend or Barry's wife or my ex-wife or anyone. Anyway, I'd given up on desks a long time ago. I get silly when I'm alone. I write in laundromats, cafes, hotel lobbies. I need the sense that there are other people doing other things, noise and laughter and hatred and money and sexual pursuit and work and more work. Donna opened up some of those possibilities. She didn't exactly push my ex-girlfriend out of my mind. She was dangerous and I was man enough to be scared. But I was definitely interested.

"All I want is to see her breasts," said Barry, twiddling his thumbs and fingers in front of his face as if he were tuning a radio set. "Come in Calcutta." That was the code for nice breasts. "Come in Berlin." He needed to talk. He was facing unemployment. The possibility of fear and hunger was getting distinct. "Just to see them, before I leave," he said. "Come in Prince George!"

But calculation applies only to hatred. We hated college administration as much as Donna hated finance company managers. These were the guys who walked the halls of the college with clip boards and beepers and had great new ideas about teaching that were all laid out on flow charts and xeroxed onto overhead transparencies so what could you say? "Do they think they can shit those kids?" said Barry. "Do they think they can control the language? They'll pay the fucking price." "Looks more like you're paying the price," I said.

"They'll pay the price," he said. "Their lives will be as stupid as they are. They think every human relationship is some kind of scam. They think it all adds up to their benefit. I won't be around to tell them different. They'll pay the price and when they do it'll be awful."

I was scared for Barry because he was going off into some world neither of us ever knew before, and he was full of new anger and wit. He was taking his family with him. It's easy to say "it'll be ok." It's easy to say "he'll be better off out of this shitpile." And I thought, with six books out, he can't really go down. He could get readings, grants. Maybe. But that doesn't count for the uncertainty, the humiliation. Joy was telling him to be a man and resign and they'd get the hell out of this stupid town. His kids were starting to have nightmares. They were peeing their beds again. They were telling their friends that their father had no job and they would have to move out of the house and be poor.

When the first-aid class ended in April, we gave Rod a bottle and went to the piano bar. When we got there, Rod told us that all the people present had passed the test. That was me and Barry, Donna and Wilma and the old guy. We drank a toast to first-aid. The old guy got more lucid. The trouble was he had a habit of talking with his elbow propped on the table and his hand flapping around and at one point he flapped my glasses right off my face and onto the next table. But we were celebrating. Rod announced that he had just been transferred out to the north end of Vancouver Island, so this was his last first-aid course in town. We had a round of toasts over that one and it turned out that the old guy had spent some time on the Island so he drew a map on his napkin of all the good fishing places. Then my house-mate Harvey came in with a swastika drawn on his tie with a felt pen and he explained that the swastika was the Sanskrit symbol for perfect happiness and offered to fight anyone who said different. We told him if he left it on we could have a real victim to work on. "What would you do," said Rod to Barry, "if you saw him lying there?" "Put the boots to him," said Barry. "My father went to war to stop those bastards." "This is a test," said Rod. "Be serious." "Check to see if the area is safe," said Barry. "Send for an ambulance. Shout in both ears, Are you alright? Are you alright?"

"No I'm not," said Harvey.

And in the course of all this I saw Donna looking at me long and wistful and damned if I didn't look the same way back at her, thinking how great it was to feel this way. If I was still married or with my girlfriend it would mean trouble, but what did it mean now? How did you, for example, move from one girl to another, your heart in two places at once?

Harvey was telling Donna to quit the finance company if she didn't like it there. Harvey's all for stepping back to see things in the larger context. At some point in the past, he stepped back and went right over the edge. He climbed back up again, though. He plants trees in the summer, goes south for a couple of months in winter to work as a stand-in disc jockey at one of the Island stations, lives mostly in the rec room at his parents' place.

Harvey and I babysit houses. If we work together we get more deals. In July and August, we babysit Barry's house while he's at the cabin. From January to April, we have a place in the downtown area. The people who own it are mutual friends who have a tax business in Dawson Creek. Actually, it's amazing how many people in this town need their houses babysat. Sometimes I'll go most of the year without paying rent. You pay the utilities and you feed the cat. Of course, only love can make a home, and home is where the heart is, but you are always being driven out of that.

When my wife first kicked me out, I learned to live around. I hung around the office. I ate out. I spent a lot of time in my car, driving the kids to piano and karate lessons. I carried toothbrush, floss, comb and bandaids in my shoulder bag. Sometimes I left the car and went into the foyers of schools to wait for the kids. I sat in the bleachers with platinum blonde mothers. I read novels, talked to janitors, watched the exercises, listened to the music. I stayed at my brother's place and Barry's. I got into babysitting houses.

I often wonder what it would be like if I had a place of my

own. I decided against it the day after I got kicked out. It was my first major decision on my own. I have a place in the country. It has a shack and some hay. Maybe that satisfies my nesting urge. I can go there whenever I have to. I could rent a place but I have two kids in high school and one in university and I want to save money for their education. In summer I spend a lot of time in the country and sometimes the kids even stay with me for a while but in winter I have no good place for them to stay, nothing like a home to offer, only strange rec rooms and bedrooms that they are not supposed to use. Love has a home, the poet says. Love cuts the lawn, puts out the garbage and pays the paper boy. These are hard skills to learn and too many different addresses don't help.

Donna was telling Harvey that she had to work to pay back a big loan. When her little sister got pregnant her parents kicked her out and she came to Donna's place. Donna was only 23 at the time and had just started at the finance company, but she looked after her sister right up to the delivery room door. "It was hell," she said. "We didn't have a cent. We hated one another. Now she's my best friend. She's back at home now and my parents think she and the kid are great and I still owe $2,000. My parents are loaded but there's no way they'll help pay it back."

"So fuck them," said Harvey.

"Yeah," she said, and then she gave me that look again.

"Want to dance?" I asked.

She nodded and we got onto the floor and waltzed a little drunkenly around, holding one another very close and she said "I knew something like this would happen."

"You sound sad," I said.

"I've got a boyfriend."

"I've got a girlfriend, sort of."

"I know. Barry told me it was all over."

"Lots of time," I said. "We could take swimming. I was reading it in the paper. Tuesday and Thursday nights, right through May and June. Barry doesn't swim. I don't swim. Do you?"

"I can't swim either."

When we got back to the table the group was splitting up. Rod gave the old guy a ride home. Donna and I proposed the swimming lessons. Wilma wasn't interested. She already had a lifeguard ticket. Harvey said he hated water. He went over to the gay bar to watch the action. The rest of us walked out together into the clear, cold air. Winter wasn't quite over. Barry said he'd register us for swimming. I walked Donna over to her car and there was another one of those long pauses. So I kissed her. Her mouth was soft and she brushed her tongue lightly against my lips. "I think we should talk," she said.

Petit Mal.

Now that I'm separated, I'm worried about relationships. Maybe I should've worried before. Actually, the word makes me puke. Actually, I've got a lot of other things to think about, so I don't worry all the time. I have to support my kid in university and look after the other two from June to January. I've got a few acres of land and a steady job. These are major accomplishments and pieces of good luck that have accrued over a long period of normal life. They make life worth living. My kid in university is going to be a nurse and look after people when they are sick or old. She writes regularly and if she doesn't I can always hold back on the cheque for a couple of days. My other two kids are into band, trail bikes, and pets. On the way to town every morning we do imitations of airline pilots with hijackers in the cockpit, and we make fun of the dj's on the local station. When they live with their mother in town I get lonely and paranoid. Of course, I have more time to think and write. I don't have to spend six hours a week in the laundromat doing a dozen pairs of jeans. I don't have to get groceries twice a week. But then I worry. When you live alone after seventeen years of marriage and jerk off by yourself once or twice a week, you start to wonder if you're still carrying a full load. You start to wonder why you're wondering.

I got a letter last week from Brenda. Three years ago

Brenda came to hear me read my stories and then we went to bed in a motel. The big bang. It was great but of course you can't do that sort of thing when you are living a relatively normal life. Maybe I needed a change. My ex-wife has a plumpish body and Brenda has a thin, nervous one. My ex-wife has very nice breasts and Brenda has hardly any. My ex-wife is a psychiatric nurse and Brenda writes surrealistic stories in the laundromat. These are the factors that change the universe.

Brenda tells me she's gone into isolation. She lives on an island and works in a quiet cafe and rents a cabin on an estuary where the swans come to nest. She swims and walks and reads. These are also the rewards of good luck and years of relative normalcy. You don't get to an island on a whim. She and her husband fought their way down through a dozen interior towns. Their marriage never made it. Her ex-husband has a live-in girlfriend so the kids generally stay with Brenda. She can't understand how her husband could go right back into another relationship. She tells me not to worry about love and sex. We both need a break. We need to be quiet. We need to wait. Eventually, something will happen and we will find someone. This is a good example of the surrealistic point of view.

The trouble is, I am in love. I've been lucky. Maybe it's the distinguished grey on my temples. Maybe it's just me. I've never been at a loss for love. I'm in love with Carol, who I met after my wife and I split up. I'm in love with Donna, who I met after Carol and I sort of split up. Of course, I'm in love with Brenda and my ex-wife too, but it seems that they are definitely in the past. Carol and Donna represent the future, and the future looks good. They are both beautiful. They are material for Hollywood dreams. I always wanted to be famous and go to Hollywood and have cocktails with Robert Redford and Jane Fonda and of course I would have a strikingly beautiful woman with me. We would have an intelligent discussion with Redford and Fonda about art. This sort of thing comes off better in Hollywood than in Canada.

I couldn't get Carol or Donna to Hollywood. They could

get there easier on their own. If they do, I hope they send me a postcard. Canada is a cold place and my art hasn't got out of bed yet. I couldn't get Donna into bed. I wasn't sure I wanted to. When I was with Carol, I couldn't even get it up. We did some great blow jobs, which is a major advantage of living in the modern age. However, fucking proves something. You assume that people in love will fuck. I haven't even tried to get Donna into bed. I don't want to get it up. I'm scared, of course, but the main problem is her boyfriend. She's in love with me, sort of, but she's in love with him, and he is young, good-looking, and has not had his vas deferens snipped. He is the future. Maybe he won't get her to Hollywood but who knows? There is lots of time for that and meanwhile there are a few other important things to think about and do.

I didn't worry when I was twenty-one. I wrote poetry and fucked my girlfriend and married her and went to university and raised kids and got jobs and travelled all across the country with family, furniture, and a dog. I did it because I was stupid. It would've been better if I'd done it because I was smart. I missed a lot, it seems, looking back. I screwed up too many times. Maybe that's why I never wrote a good poem. I wasn't thinking. I'm glad I did it anyway. But now that I'm over forty I want to know what I'm doing. I want Donna in bed and in my stories. Or Carol, if she comes back to me, if Donna marries her boyfriend and moves to Smithers.

You are not supposed to have options, you are supposed to be in love. No wonder I couldn't get it up. Maybe I'm worn out after seventeen years of blind potency. Maybe I'm tired. Maybe I was never meant to be a lover. As it turns out, I'm a much better father. All through my life, I've had trouble acting instinctively. I have faded emotions. I have slow reactions. Sometimes I have no reactions at all. This goes back a long way. I remember one time my sister, just a baby, rolled down the front steps of the house. I was coming up, a boy back from school, and I just let her roll by. My parents were surprised. I remember my younger brother, learning to ride a bike, heading straight for the house, so frightened he was still pedalling. My girlfriend had to run out to stop him. I remember once when I was a student, I was sitting in a bar with friends on the day that Kennedy was shot. I was saying that I never really liked the guy (I might have said "asshole") when a guy got up from the next table, dragged me out of my chair and slapped me across the face. I just looked at him. I felt he had acted well.

I hate stories about the day Kennedy was shot. Every liberal has one. How sad, to identify with his sordid life, even if he was maybe among the best of them, our days measured by the evening news. He went all the way and of course he had to murder to do it, but he mouthed our ideals anyway and that made us proud. That's our big problem. That's our main weakness. We know that our ideals are hopeless but we don't want to hear it. We will do anything not to hear it. We hate conservatives. They believe that the truth gives you power. They love power. It is more important than people. They make decisions and carry them out and when they are happy you can be sure that someone is bleeding. We don't want to hurt anyone. We want to believe in ourselves and others. However, we can't quite do it. We are afraid. We want protection. We want power. We have to hurt people to get it. We hate the people who are hurting. They cannot see how sorry we are. We hate the legendary lovers who own the world because they don't need it. They can walk away from it as if it were nothing. They aren't going to tell us anything but the truth and we know it. We don't want to hear it. "We must love one another or die," the poet says. You first, Bill. We hate ourselves. That is how you feel when you know the truth.

Carol thought I was burnt out. She wanted joy, innocence, friendship and was willing to fight for them. She had a rough life. Donna thinks I have a low opinion of myself. She is afraid. She is the kind of person you can talk to. She would rather talk than fight. She would rather fight than fuck, unless conditions are right, and they are seldom or maybe never right. She knows all about my problem. When we were taking first-aid, we spent a lot of time together drinking wine, taking one another's pulse, and comparing symptoms. She figures I'm allergic to my own adrenalin. I could be in the early stages of MS.

The fact is, I don't want to be cured. I'm too old. I'll carry on with my infirmities until they threaten to kill me. Notice I didn't say "until they kill me." I love the twitching prostate that gets me up at midnight. How else would I see midnight? Probably I love my impotence too. After all, every few nights for three months I got to come into the mouth of one of the world's most beautiful women. I was spoiled. Of course I would've liked to fuck her. Blow jobs get a bit clinical after a while. Besides, I imagine if I had fucked her I'd still have her in my bed, be in her bed, drink coffee with her on Sunday morning or walk with her and her little boy to the park. But maybe not. Probably not. She says not, but she's just trying to make me feel better.

This could be my future. I've noticed recently that I sometimes blank out when I reach orgasm. Liberalism is insinuating itself into my sex life. Nothing is sacred. Everything is sacred. This is not too good because I miss a few crucial strokes. Some day maybe I'll pass out as soon as I reach for it. I wonder what would happen if someone else were doing the stroking. I could tell Donna about this and maybe she'd be curious, but I don't think so. She's a loan officer at the finance company and that requires a certain formality, and things like rape, the economy, the plight of the indian and individual happiness concern her very deeply.

Donna was raised on a Saskatchewan farm among the usual perverts who live out there. Her mother made sure that she or her sister never sat on Grandfather's lap. Her uncle was put in the can for molesting kids. When she got older, some guy made regular trips into the farmyard at night. "I never could tell if my parents were serious about finding out who it was," she says. "I always had a suspicion they knew. One night my Dad and brother tracked the guy to the woodlot and they stood there firing their rifles into the bush. What the hell good was that supposed to do? They could've killed him." Donna also claims she was odd one out all through school.

"The women hated me. I had a mouth on me. I was popular with the boys because I had breasts. Jesus did I have breasts. By the time I was thirteen we had to go to Regina for bras. You should've heard the jokes at the Co-op. I was a major consideration for all the boys. That's all they do out there. They wear hats and they throw rocks and they look at breasts. Actually I was ugly. My legs were like sticks and my two front teeth are crooked."

"Funny I never noticed," I said.

Donna has had some weird relationships. She says she wants to get married and have kids. She says she's tried hard. One guy stuck her in a mobile home in a mining camp, worked twelve hours a day and always came home with a case of beer and a buddy. Another guy beat her up when she left him. She passed out when he got her down on the bed and started choking her. The last thing she thought was, this is it. She says she didn't feel too bad about it. Just a few weeks ago, the guy who's training her in loan management showed up at her place one night, hung around so long she finally had to tell him she wasn't interested. He was insulted and slammed the door on his way out. The next day at work she felt like a shit and apologized and he said forget it. But a week later a rumour was going around that he laid her. He told her about the rumour, and told her not to worry about it, it didn't bother him, and she said "why the fuck would it bother you?" This is not the way to move ahead in the loan department.

Donna tells lots of stories like this. They are questions and threats. I think she's best off with her boyfriend, as happy as she'll be with any guy except me. "We have it out in the open," she says. "Actually, we probably spend half the time fighting. I think it's good to sort it out as you go."

"Yeah," I said. "My wife and I never did that."

"You were too sneaky, right?"

"But not sneaky enough."

"Why didn't you just talk to her? It seems a shame you had to go and blow it all up in order to get what you want. You could've just talked it out."

"What did I want?"

"If you'd talked, maybe you would've figured it out, dummy."

The trouble with Donna's boyfriend is he's eight years younger than her and comes from a big family. They spend a lot of time visiting. They sit at the kitchen table and drink tea and talk about cars. They have Sunday dinners and the women wash the dishes and the men go into the living room. Donna got tired of it. She didn't want to talk to her future brother-in-law's wife all the time. She claims she's always gotten along better with men anyway, except when they try to kill her. She started going into the living room too, but her boyfriend asked her not to do that. His parents freak out. She went along because he's not into male stereotypes when he's away from his family.

He's a quiet guy, like me. Of course, that could be only on the surface, like me. Actually, my dreams and fantasies are extremely violent. This could be the result of self-hatred. This is something that I don't have to hide from Donna. One time when I was riding in her car she flipped out because a guy was driving too slow in front of her. She was swearing, pounding on the steering wheel and stamping her feet on the floor. I was glad to see this because I do it too. Of course, I have to be careful because sometimes I blank out. I've assassinated politicians, kicked asshole kids down stairs, and beat up each one of my oldest daughter's boyfriends, all in my fantasies. I love TV detective stories with car chases, World War II footage, that same Stuka hitting the grey Atlantic. Suck cod water, Fritz! My ex-wife believed that these fantasies reveal a frustration and paranoia that is not entirely innocent but shows itself in other ways – impatience, petulance, sarcasm, character assassination. I do have a bad mouth. Of course, she is using her professional knowledge to legitimize leaving me. For her, my fling with Brenda is losing its proportions. For me, the proportions are getting bigger all the time.

You have to know what you want. That's what I tell Donna. Enough guys have pumped enough sperm into her to produce a kid, but no kid. Of course, she's woman enough to be scared, and it's easy for me to talk about it. I went at it blind and was lucky and now I'm almost finished. When you have kids, you hardly need anyone else, and Donna would like that. Also, when I was very young I wanted to be a poet. I tried it for years and was generally unsuccessful but I never gave up until I started writing and publishing stories. Donna likes my stories. She says that English was her best course in school. The trouble is, my life is tied down. I know where I'm going. Nowhere, but at least I'm on the road. At worst, I suffer loneliness and boredom.

Donna finds me calm. She likes me for this. She feels easy. She tells me she wants me. She tells me she doesn't know what to do. I like her desperation, the fact that she won't give in to it and she won't give it up. She's all wit and sensitivity and maybe that's her fate. She's a noble woman. Her eyes have been opened, and she so young. When she holds my hand and tells me she wants me and doesn't know what to do, I tell her not to worry. "You're safe with me," I say.

Clearcut.

If anything worries me it's the thought that my kids will soon be on their own. Not that I won't be proud. Not that I'd never see them. But a family is a family, and when the kids go away, it's over. Maybe if I wasn't separated I wouldn't be so worried. My wife and I could count on lives of mutual support. That's what we originally had in mind. Of course, one of us would've croaked first, and the other would have to go into the Sunset Lodge alone, but at least we could've put in a decade or two together. Unfortunately, calculation doesn't entirely determine these things, and I blew the marriage, so that ends that, and there's no way you can keep the kids around. Maybe there'll be a depression and they'll all come back to the family farm.

The best thing about waking up on the farm, especially on weekends, is that they're upstairs in their cosy rooms under their cosy down blankets. Makes you want to get up, put another log on the fire, and whip up some pancakes. The trouble is you can't do that, because then you'd have to wake them all up to eat the pancakes, and chances are one or two or all of them would rather sleep. So you just put another log on the fire. The best thing about living on a farm is seeing them play golf in the pasture or go fishing in the creek, breathing that fresh air and hearing nothing but quiet. Even though they are inordinately attached to trail bikes, TV, and radio rock music, at least they've got both worlds and, in this world, the more worlds the better.

I dream about my kids, about their being here and going away. I dream only when I'm alone, and in my dreams I am always alone. I'm asleep in one of the upstairs bedrooms, where I sometimes sleep when my kids are staying in town with their mother. The floors are warm up there. I dream that I hear my kids come up the road and into the yard, they are talking out in front of the house, wondering if I am around. For some reason they don't come in. Maybe the door is locked, and after a while they leave, and I hear their voices get further away. I struggle to get up, to call after them, but there is a great weight on my chest and arms, and I can't open my eyes or my mouth.

Lennie Bruce once said that when you leave your wife you spend the first two years puking. I didn't have to spend that long. I still had a family to hold onto. I have to hold onto my job until my kids are all into university. If I can't hold onto my job, I'll sell the farm. The kids get angry when I talk about this, because the farm is their home, and once a year they walk out into the trees. We have a hundred acres of pine, some parts of it very mature so there is hardly any undergrowth and the dead have almost disappeared into the ground. The trees are quiet and stately. The local loggers cast covetous eyes on them whenever they go past in their pickups. Sometimes they come up our bumpy road to say they are logging nearby and now's the time to make a good deal. I give them coffee and they give the kids some half-used cans of fluorescent paint or a few half-rolls of surveyor's tape. They tell me that a mature stand can only lose value. Someday, my trees will have to pay. The loggers know. It's their job. Someday, one way or another, the trees will get sold. They cannot be permitted to live their lives out, generation after generation, locked in their green circles of light.

They are safe this winter. I cashed in five thousand dollars of paid-up life insurance and got Victoria into first-year Nursing at the University of British Columbia. UBC is my Alma Mater. I never went back for almost twenty years after I graduated, but I contributed twenty-five dollars a year to the fund. Every few months I get their magazine and flip through it in a mild kind of wonder, looking for something familiar. It is a PR magazine. The only negative thing you ever see in it is the "Deaths" column where you discover that a bachelor's or master's or even a doctoral degree does not mean immortality. You discover that the vast majority of alumni pass their lives in total obscurity and never do anything more than run small engineering consultant firms or teach for forty years in high schools or spend three years in Angola showing the people how to pay the national debt. Some of them are barely across the street, the ink still wet on their parchment, when they are hit.

The rest of the alumni magazine is mainly devoted to the discoveries and adventures of the administration, faculty, and grad students. Someone is going to Africa to dig up bones. Someone is spending a month in the high Arctic studying seal migration. So what? Let them do the study and publish the results. I don't want to hear about other people's prospects and adventures. The trees are paying for it all. It might be ten thousand dollars tossed down a blowhole in the ice for all I know. If a new building goes up it is paid for by a few thousand acres of standing pine. Compared to a few thousand acres of standing pine, the building is a shitpile. Let's have a little respect and let's not pretend we are doing a great job when we are just doing a job.

Sometimes, though, in the pages of the magazine, I find that one of my fellows is not dead or not pretending to be alive but is indeed living (or has indeed lived) a life of accomplishment. There was an article on George Bowering a few years ago, on his books of poetry and prose, and I knew about George Bowering when I was at university though of course being a young intellectual I thought he was a shithead. I went to one of his readings and it was not like Lord Byron. My friend Bill, a Commonwealth Exchange Student (white) from Kenya, said "Yeah, fucking bullshit man!" and we went to the cafeteria and got coffees and talked about our own work which really was bullshit. Now I read everything by Bowering I can get my hands on (which is enough to break you) and I send in my twenty-five dollars and I tell my kids that UBC is ok if they want to go there.

I'm still attached to the free pursuit of learning. I fancy the trees don't mind paying for that. I like the idea of putting people and good books together. Of course, most people, even young people, are too uptight to freely pursue anything but money. Even the university has backed off, though it didn't want to. It has old ideas too and besides "the free pursuit of learning" doesn't commit you to anything definite, like work. Victoria is booked into twenty-seven hours a week of class and lab time. With homework, that's like basic training. But she still reads Donne in her English class. "Death be not proud, though some have called thee / Mighty and dreadful for thou art not so." What has that got to do with Nursing? Aren't there more relevant things to study? Besides, apart from the obvious meaning, and in a loose translation, it means "Look at me! You boring assholes will have to shit blood to learn how to do this," the eternal message of all art. No wonder people hate it. They are ashamed of their desperate need to understand and excel. They may go to the bar and let the musicians play for them while they dance drunkenly around or they may read a few books or go to the movies or even the opera if they are high class, but when the Gestapo marches in the first thing they do is turn in their neighbourhood musicians, poets, painters. Here they are, the ones who betrayed us. Burn them. They are worse than criminals, traitors, communists. They told us the biggest lie of all. They told us we could live.

I went back to UBC just before Christmas to pick Victoria up. It turned out that her residence is the same one I was in. Now they call it something else. It looks the same, though a bit worse for wear. You can go right into the women's dorms. I stood in the foyer like a jerk trying to find some way of ringing up Victoria's room. The switchboard was gone. A teenage guy went cruising right through the foyer and up the stairs. When some girls came out I explained how I'd come for my daughter and asked how do I get to her and they said (laughing) "you go up and knock on her door."

Before we left the campus she showed me the new bookstore and the sunken library which is very nice though I'm not much into books anymore except a few. She showed me the Student Union Building and the swimming pool. Later, when we got to my parents' place, the newspaper had an article by Eric Nicol about the man who was President of the University when I was there. My mother showed the article to me and reminded me that, on the day of my graduation, when she and my dad were on campus, they met the President in an elevator and he was very interested in them and me. He said it was great that a longshoreman's son got a degree. It was a magic moment for them. This man was President for years and of course I thought he was a shithead, but Nicol, who is also an alumni and one of the living ones, said he was the last of the Presidents known to have a personality. There were some old photos of him in uniform being visited by Lord Mountbatten who I also thought was a shithead but everyone now, especially since he and his yacht were blown to shit by the IRA, says that he had a personality. There was an old photo of the President in cap and gown with football shorts and brawny knees, one foot resting expertly on the ball, and the photo was rumoured to have shocked the Dean of Women at the time. I doubt this but anyway the Dean of Women was cut a few years back as a budgetary measure. That probably did shock her. I didn't read about this in the alumni magazine or Eric Nicol. There was a recent picture of the President in his fishing hat sitting in a boat with a rod in his hand and he looks old. All I know is that Eric Nicol says the President had a personality and my mother, who has a personality that Eric Nicol would notice but not write about, liked the President when she met him in an elevator.

I think that if the President did have a personality he would be a sad man. My mother likes sad men. Nicol doesn't mention any sadness in his article. I assume that's what's missing. Personality doesn't go with success. A university is not endowed to build personality. If it was, it would be a forest. Civilization hates personality. Civilization is the gang rape of nature and human nature. Personality cries out against it. Sometimes personality uses the voice of art. People confuse art and civilization but they are opposites. Civilization hates personality unless it is dead or almost dead (like the President). It wants to cut it up and analyze and use it. It wants to know what to expect. Sometimes it is well-meaning but mostly it is scared silly. It cannot deal with every living individual. It cannot satisfy that desire.

In Canada, there are 2.5 people on every square mile of land. The .5 person is the mayor. This person does not believe in whole numbers. This makes him very efficient. He is not a dreamer. He does not want anything that you can't win in a lottery. He gets elected by convincing one of the two whole numbers that the other is actually the .5 person. This is fundamental to all political action. The person the mayor convinces is the Voter. Voters are not fractions, but they are able to live like them. They are "nice." They own .25 of a house, drive .5 of a car, have 1.3 kids and are relatively happy. They dream of wholeness at 65 years of age. They are the backbone of civilization. They belong to parties, support charities, watch the news and suffer angst. Given a bar of soap and told to line up for a shower, they are convinced by the time they reach the head of the line that they need a shower and are going to get one. Most of the time they are right.

The other whole person is the Indian. Indians don't believe in fractions and can't learn to live like them. They don't vote. They refuse to believe that Germans stink, young people can't think or write, civil servants are lazy, and communists evil. They have the ability to walk away from half houses, cars etc. They will not volunteer for active duty, join the administration, or support a party, charity, or church of your choice. They fall in love and stay there, write poetry or paint pictures.

They are over the edge. Given a bar of soap and told to take a shower, they know that something is wrong. Usually they are right.

I was a Voter but maybe I'm turning into an Indian. I'm having trouble appraising my situation. I used to teach poetry at the college where I work. That was alright, given that I don't like working. I like the money. Then they told me that, in times of fiscal restraint and social crisis, it was inappropriate to teach poetry to young people. I was told that my life-long efforts in that direction had failed to resolve certain problems that young people have with thinking and writing. As a matter of fact, I was a major cause of those problems. However, they didn't fire me. They were very understanding. They were willing to overlook my literary activity. They said that my experience could still, possibly, be of value. They put me in the Centre.

When students come to the college they are given a multiple-choice writing test. A computer in Boston marks this test and informs them as to their deficiencies. Then the students bring these results to me in the Centre. I present them with certain (colour-coded) exercise books, which in turn refer them to certain texts, video-cassettes, and floppy discs, each item keyed to the test and designed to help the student with his or her particular deficiencies. The students complete these exercises and I help them monitor their progress. When they are finished they take another multiple-choice test. This one is marked in Toronto. In this way, they learn only what they need to learn and are not saddled with extraneous social, cultural, and personal baggage. They do not have to listen to me talk about Bowering, Conrad, Donne, or my divorce. Also, they are graded by objective standards. Personality does not come into it.

The Centre is brightly lit. There are computers with user-friendly programs. They are very polite and patient. There is a coffee machine and a Coke machine. The secretaries, Pat and Betty, keep track of materials and monitor attendance. I mark, file, and record completed exercises and review new materials. I like the black people in the American video lessons. They look happy and healthy, like they get lots of sun and vegetables. They walk with their arms around the white people and laugh. The Stars and Stripes is radiant above them, flowing in a clear sky. There is a picture of Martin Luther King on the classroom wall. They knit their brows and pucker up their faces and write. They write about meaningful issues. It seems like a lot of fun. There are a couple of black people at the college but in this town it is mainly whites and indians. There are a few indians in the Centre but they don't laugh or smile, not even when they see the black people looking cute and putting their arms around white people.

Victoria thinks I should quit. She says I am wasting my time working for the fuckfaces who run the college. She says the administration is a dumping ground for psychos. It makes her very nervous when she comes to the Centre to see me. I'm proud of her because she is tough-minded, apart from the army of teddy-bears she lives with, some of which are always being kidnapped and held for ransom by the Engineers. "How can you do that shit?" she says. "How can you work with those droolers? How can you give up your ideas?" I remind her that I am not adept at living amongst the trees. I can't soak up nourishment from the ground. Besides, she needs money to become a nurse. "Remember," I say, "don't get off the boat." This is a private joke. From time to time, we say it to one another. "Stay on the fucking boat. Be a teacher. Be a nurse. Don't get off the boat!"

She worries about my private life too. She doesn't want me to be alone. She gets angry at Jen and Wes for spending more and more time in their mother's house in town and less and less time with me on the farm. She wants me to marry Carol or Donna and go to Mexico or Hollywood. I'd sit on the beach and write great literature or drink coffee with Redford and Fonda and then Carol or Donna would come from work and we would go out to dinner and then to the movies or a party and then come home and fuck until dawn. She's mad because I let Carol go. She wants me to do something about Donna. "I think she's in love with you," she says. "To hell with her boy-friend. That's her problem. Besides, I kind of like him my-self."

I tell her I'm ok. I may look old, but there's still lots of time. My friends look after me. I tell her how Donna came back from Kamloops a month ago, just for a visit. We had some very sophisticated breakfasts together. We drank coffee until noon. Then I went to work and Donna went over to Joy's and they had vodkas until dinner. They decided I had to get off the farm. I could saw my leg off, walk into a family of hungry coyotes at night, blow myself up trying to start the truck with the propane heater. Jen and Wes would not be around to get hungry and come looking for me. Clayton came over while they were drinking and he had a few vodkas with them and mentioned that his girlfriend was going south to UBC in Jan-uary to do a course in Art Therapy. Her studio in the base-ment would be empty. I could rent it for $150 per month.

"Are you going to do it?" asked Victoria.

I said I would. I need the company. I'll wander around town, eat a few cafe meals, continue my swimming lessons. It'll be easier to get to work. I wish I was more independent, though. I wish I could live at the edges, the abandoned places. But it's too hard. Maybe it's unnatural. On the Berlin Wall it says, "Be like a tree, alone in the brotherhood of the forest." Nice try, Ernst, but those cathedral groves are Passchendaeles. Those stately pines, like the Allies at Potsdam, have the sap of hundreds on their hands. They shade each other out. The losses are incredible. The ones that die feed the ones that live. It's the way they're made. They can't think of a way out. There's no end of sun, but not nearly enough to go around.

Living with Clayton.

One day when I got to the college, Don had a copy of *University Affairs* and in it he'd circled a job at York in Toronto and he said "if you don't apply for this, and get the hell off this shitpile, I'm going to give up on you." Don is a serious academic and for the last couple of years he has managed what there is left of our departmental business. Barry and I can't do it. We've occupied what's left of our minds elsewhere. The rest of the department is either spooked or comatose. We are managing the last bridgehead of the Humanities in a northern town. Casualties have been heavy. French, Spanish, History, Music, Theatre, Creative Writing and Philosophy are dead. Dacum charts are posted everywhere. Managers fly to Japan or the Appalachian School of Developmental Studies. There is a sense of the end of civilization as we know it. Don figures that an organized retreat is in order. We get our asses back to headquarters.

I took the magazine to my office and pretended to give it serious consideration. I knew Don would also apply for this job. He would write me a letter and I would write him a letter. Sometimes this doesn't look too good, but we've both been at this place for some time and have no other alternatives since the managers have all gone over and think we are jerks. Don wants to go east but I don't. He's from there, a hillbilly

Ukrainian from Thunder Bay, whereas I am from Vancouver. I don't want to be so far away from my kids. I don't like Eastern weather and acid rain. I don't like big cities. I have no reason to go except that my working life could end here at an inconvenient time. Last year, Barry's almost did, but we got a letter campaign going and went on CBC and they gave him his job back. Besides, my humanistic conscience is starting to bother me. I always thought if I was a Nazi soldier I would refrain from stuffing anyone in an oven even if it meant my life, but around here I am telling students all the time that orders are orders.

However, I'm not going to apply. I'm going to stick it out. I don't like the idea of being in a fortress. The college is bad enough. Universities look good from the outside. The gardens are well-tended and the buildings are warm and there are lots of places to sit and think. However, the outside world is too far away. The people inside are involved in serious miscalculations about the most serious things. They write poetry and discuss it with one another in faggoty voices on the CBC. When Don was at UBC he devoted his creative hours to the poetry of Bliss Carman. This is natural for a bootlegger's son fresh out of the bush. Carman is ok if you want to practise the rudiments of academic technique. However, Don might have persevered in it, if he hadn't landed a job and come north in the heyday of our college's growth. The new building had just arisen from the gravel in the light industrial area of town, close to the by-pass where the trucks roll north to the Alaska Highway. The portable buildings were bulldozed and burned. It seemed like a victory for sweetness and light and only the veterans had a sense of foreboding. Fortresses are hard to defend. It gets so the walls are the only thing you can trust. You can't trust anyone who is not inside. Finally, you can't trust anyone.

Barry and I were always suspect. Barry never was an academic. He is a musician and a poet. He has a degree in psychology and worked in Vancouver as a social worker. He quit that and went into creative writing. At night he delivered pizzas. He got his degree but there were no jobs. He hung around the Vancouver jazz clubs playing his drums and writing poetry. Joy worked in the public library. They were close to starvation when the Principal of the college came down to the city to recruit faculty. The college was brand new then, a row of portables set on cement blocks around the old Vocational School. There were colour photos of it on the wall in the Hotel Vancouver conference room that the Principal had rented. "It looked like a fucking logging camp," said Barry. "What got me the job was that I didn't smoke. There was this room with pictures, this bald guy with a very German accent. As a matter of fact, it turned out he was an officer on a Nazi sub during the war. Anyway, in this room in the hotel there was a table and two chairs and the table was clear except for one thing – a package of cigarettes. No ashtray. He asked me if I wanted a cigarette and I said no. I found out later it was a test. If you smoked you didn't get a job. I was smoking three packs a day at the time. I was grabbing half-finished smokes off the sidewalk and bumming off everyone."

I came from a prairie college. That was my first job after McGill. I could've worked at a university but I thought I'd try a college, see if it was more interesting. Besides, my wife and I wanted to live in a small town. We wanted out of the big cities. We had three little kids and were concerned about their health. However, the prairies were a mistake. I should've figured it out, but I was a Vancouver boy so what did I know? The administration and faculty there wore suits and cowboy boots. The cowboy boots didn't have any shit on them. I don't have Barry's instincts. When I got there I discovered that most of them were Mormons. By December I had my walking papers. I said "fuck" in class a thousand times too often. I couldn't help it. When I was going to university I worked summers as a longshoreman. I learned how to swear.

When Barry came to the college he started a literary magazine. This was part of his job. Apparently, fascists support the arts. They prefer things that are over a hundred years old, but they realize that when you are on the frontier you have to start somewhere. By the time I came to the college, Barry was into mimeo chapbooks. Unfortunately, the Principal left that year. He got into a fight with the local capitalists. It seems that they don't like the arts no matter how old they are. I brought my own magazine from the prairies and got some money from the Canada Council for more printing equipment. Barry got a government grant to pay students to work through the summer. Eventually, we had a full-scale print room in a warehouse on the edge of campus. We were flooding the town with poetry. The people we published came up and gave readings. We had conferences and drank lots of beer. The visiting writers had a great time drinking and reading. Sometimes they even fucked the friendly locals or vice versa. We went on for five years like that while the college grew. The management grew too. They couldn't figure out what we were doing. The doors were wide open. The lights were on all night. The print room was full of ecologists, feminists, and other weirdos. The public was asking questions. Soon, we were out of business. They gave up the warehouse and we took our equipment away. We didn't say much. At least they didn't fire us. We figured we could work out of our basements. We were getting tired of being responsible. If the town didn't want the business and the PR and all the exciting cultural activities provided by our genius, then fuck them. You can't fight city hall. It was getting bigger than the both of us. We were moved into a windowless office in the new building, our desks crammed together face-to-face and the shelves crammed with dozens of useless composition and rhetoric texts. On the first day there, Barry brought in two ties that he got at the Sally-Ann. We put them on and concentrated on teaching English to Forestry students. Nobody else wanted them. They were mostly older and they knew all about the long skidder road of life. They had shoved their butts into the debarker of experience. They had matched their Stihls against the northern forest. They said, "Jesus Christ, sir, do we have to learn this shit again?" They saved our lives.

I can't imagine myself at York University, assuming I could get the job, which is not likely. I would have twelve hours a week of classes instead of twenty-five. I would have students who would not write "the chainsaw is busted." They would believe in freedom of thought and would know how to get ahead by saying yes. It's that kind of arrogance that can get you a long way and then very quickly get you killed. I would have colleagues and superiors who had retained their faith in themselves along with their mortgages, pension payments, and music lessons for the kids. They had never gone outside the walls after dark, never been yelled at, shit-kicked, and pissed on. At the college, this is an everyday event.

Of course, I can still understand Don's point of view. You get tired of sitting in the corners of bars trying to have serious conversations about poetry and wondering if someone is going to pour a beer down your back. The local theatre group does *My Fair Lady* for the third year in a row. The orchestra has a guest musician every year but the urinals in the adjoining gym cough up the town reservoir every five minutes and the stage hands from the sponsoring hardware store with cigarette packs rolled in their sleeves drop the lid on the piano.

I tell Don that his attitude is naive. There are advantages. You can walk to any of a dozen bars in ten minutes and for the price of a beer watch a beautiful lady or guy if you prefer take off his/her clothes or you can hear some new Vegas act working its way north to the oil rigs in the Beaufort Sea. You can promenade in the shopping centre with no coat or boots on and buy Nabokov's *Complete Works* (hardcover) in one volume for $1.99. You can go to the public library and the only books missing are the doctor-nurse ones from the new paperback shelves. You can make contact with the local artists who move around town in flak jackets and steel-toed boots and talk about the city, and you can study their art and figure out who will be famous. You can do some of these things in the city too but if you are in the fortress why would you bother? It wouldn't help your career. The more real fighting you do, the more you look like the enemy. A job is great that way if you are tough enough to really do it. It will take you exactly where you have to be in order to think and write clearly – up Moloch's asshole, up the Congo to the Inner Station. No one can just imagine it.

My landlord Clayton had this opportunity. He made it to the end. He was hauled into the Dean's office and terminated. He was told that History was history. The Dean pointed out that, in times of fiscal restraint, it is inappropriate for so many students to be taking university courses. Education should be job-oriented. Students would need technological expertise to face the future. Clayton didn't say much at that point. He knew that you don't argue with history, at least not without considerable forethought.

Now he is writing a novel while his UI runs out and the real estate people parade their clients through the house. He is taking a big risk. He asks me about novels and I just shrug. I could no more write a novel than I could pay my Chargex. What keeps him going is necessity and intellectual arrogance. He is still young. He wasn't at the college that long. His degree is still relatively fresh. He gets up at 7 AM and showers and has a boiled egg and bean sprouts on toast and goes to work. He smokes and listens to CBC. He works until mid-afternoon and then walks his dog. I admire him. If I were in his circumstances I would be getting up late and sitting in a cafe staring at my coffee until the bar opened.

Clayton is justifiably angry. His courses were popular. Before he finished the semester he took on the college and the students supported him. There was a protest and letters to the editor. Clayton wrote a few articles. The Dean was angry. He summoned Clayton to his office. "I think you should step back and take a look at yourself," he said. Clayton stood back and looked. His fly was done up. His shirt was tucked in. "What am I supposed to see?" he asked. He was supposed to see the necessity of taking a walk. He was supposed to get serious. Instead, he wanted to ask questions. That, in the present crisis state of the western world, is considered traitorous. There is no time for any discussion of the larger issues. The Dean is highly paid to produce solutions to the crisis, and you can't produce solutions if you don't believe in the crisis. Clayton was saying that there is always a crisis but it is not usually the one people think it is. History is an important clue. Public figures don't want to hear that kind of academic bullshit. They have their so-called lives to live.

Barry and I do a lot of writing so we are pretty reserved about Clayton's chances with the novel. We don't want to prejudice his luck, but life is short and art is long etc., and finally hardly anyone really cuts it. We don't want to read his novel either. The problem is that Clayton, having been thrown out of the fort, is trying to write his way back in. If that sort of thing works, Barry and I are fucked and what you are reading now is shit.

My new girlfriend Alison can't see why it can't work. She doesn't mind talking to Clayton about his novel. She is eager to read it. For her it is an interesting development and a practical consideration. She has never met a novelist before. She thinks that being a novelist is better than being a History instructor. Clayton was lucky he got laid off. Alison thinks the college is ok even without History and the printshop. It will get her into pre-med. Besides, she likes Clayton. He is very graceful whenever she and I decide to spend the night together in my little room in the basement. In the morning when we get up he is having coffee and we have some with him and he and Alison talk about the novel before we go off to the college.

Clayton likes her. He asks me about her and I answer. Maybe he is writing her into his novel. If he is, I would like to read it. He asks me if her husband knows what is going on and I say yes. When Alison figured she wanted to have an affair with me she sat down and had a talk with him and they arrived at an understanding. They have been married for a long time and get along very well. I was uncomfortable at first, especially when I found out that her husband actually knew my name and place of work. Barry figured he probably works behind the ammo counter in the local hardware store. He said, "It sounds pretty weird." "He could come up to me some time and wreck my face," I said to Alison. "You can always tell me to fuck off," she said. I decided it was worth taking a chance. Sex is important. I trusted her. She gave me a book to bring me up to date on sexual mores. She told me she would refrain from inviting me to affairs where her husband and I might meet. "It's a shame, though," she said. "He really wants to meet you."

The book explained that permanent relationships are important but they should not exclude those temporary ones that can satisfy those needs that may not be met by permanent ones. Of course, it seems that the needs provided for by temporary relationships are mainly sexual, but the book didn't go into that. It advocated total honesty with people. I figured, it's got to be better than the approach I used when I was married. Besides, I was curious to see if I was still impotent. When Alison made an appointment to meet me at the bar one night I figured she wanted to sleep with me. I kissed her when she dropped me off at my place. She was surprised. "Why did you do that?" she asked. "To make you comfortable," I said. I wasn't afraid. I knew I could rise into love with her. You can tell these things when you are not being stupid.

Sometimes I am jealous of her husband. She commutes home to him on weekends. They lie together in bed and talk about the future. Their kids come in with coffee. They have a great life. They haven't fooled around. Alison was only eighteen when she had their first kid. They ran a garage together and made enough to go to Greece for two months. Then her husband's arm was crushed when the lift fell on him. It took a long time for him to come out of that. They sold the garage and she worked in a doctor's office and he sold used cars. Their kids went through school. Their parents got old. They did what they had to do. They have a past. I'm lucky she needed a brief encounter with me. She likes my face. She likes my stories. She even likes me in bed. She asks if I only pretended to be impotent so I could write the stories. She says that if Carol or Donna come back to me she will step aside. She figures that by the time she leaves for university I will really know how to fly again. I tell her that I can only fly with her. With someone else I will have to learn it all over again. Maybe I won't be able to. "That will make for a lot of stories," she said.

Alison has booked me until the end of the semester. After that I can return to my platonic affairs with Carol and Donna, only then I'll have to add Alison to the list. I'm getting the sense that things are coming to an end, that I should get the hell out of here before I am all alone and while I can still move. But I can't. It's hard to explain, but when I was a young man in Vancouver working the docks I used to stand on the decks of the ships and look across Burrard Inlet to those mountains and I used to think, someday I'm going to see what's on the other side. I thought, that is my country too. I imagined quiet lakes, intimate settlements, lonely cabins, and the forest. Eventually I made it and now I want to stay.

Harvey understands. He is a native. He loves this place. He has gone away and come back a number of times. "You can survive," he says. When I worry about not having a job to get my kids to university he says "there are all kinds of jobs for you." Of course, he said this after we'd been in the bar for three hours. He has been a journeyman printer, a disc jockey, a tree-planter, a mailman, and now he is trying to get on as assistant coroner. He is the only "poet" to be short-listed. The present coroner has taken a shine to him. Once they went to an autopsy together. It was part of the test to get the job. The corpse was a faller and he had suicided by sticking his head in the bite of a tree as it came down. When the coroner asked what he thought, Harvey said that he had to admire the guy. The coroner agreed. "One of the best ones I've ever seen," he said. "Real class."

The trouble is, in this world you are expected to go all the way. You are not expected to attach yourself to an idea, or a person, or a town, or a piece of ground. People who do that are dreamers. They do not want to go any further. They think they have seen enough. They figure they have the general idea. The forests will be cut down or poisoned. The people will be cut down or poisoned. Alison figures my perspective is overly pessimistic. She thinks I could use a change. She is eager to get into medicine. She sleeps five hours a night, smokes a pack and a half a day, and drinks ten cups of coffee. She worries about my lack of enthusiasm. She can put up with a cool lover because she has a warm husband, but she figures I could be replaced in my job by someone who is more hopeful. Young people need that. But who will sort out the truth, such as it is, assuming that it is, assuming those things that people think when they suffer and die? Who will teach them how to fail? Maybe Clayton will.

Maybe I've gone far enough. I sure hope so. I've got a good imagination. Sometimes it's too good. When I decided that I didn't need sex anymore, I got it. If I put off writing the story long enough, I write it. I am on the other side of the mirror, staring out, untouchable, cold. I have replaced ambition with a vague yearning. This makes me attractive but only because I have grey hair at the temples and look sexy in dark glasses. Fortunately, most people are too busy to embrace art. Their world is blood-warm and spastic and if they often look at the mirror it is only to straighten a tie or apply lipstick or make sure their blood is not outside their skin. They are not curious. Alison is getting curious and it is worrying her. She is writing too, even though she's supposed to concentrate on her studies. Most people know that they will go through the mirror soon enough. They will lose out in love and radio music will fill their eyes with vague tears. They will look into their doctor's eyes and read failure. They will watch their children run towards failure. They will run out of brains or tricks. They will sicken and die.

When we lie together in bed, Alison draws on her cigarette and looks at me with her big blue eyes and asks "are you happy?" and I say "yes" and she says "I wonder" and upstairs Clayton's typewriter rumbles like distant thunder. She finishes her cigarette and reaches for another and lights it. She draws on it thoughtfully. "He's having trouble with the sex scene," she says.

My Heart
is a Red Volkswagen.

This summer I am at Barry and Joy's house. I might spend
two or three days a week out on the farm, painting or cutting hay, and then I come to town and have a shower and
watch videos. Barry and Joy's place is a very old house for this
town, built by a mill owner at the turn of the century, and it is
on the town's most dignified street. The people from the historical society are trying to save it by having it proclaimed a
heritage house, and they often come around in the morning
when I am sitting at the kitchen table with a pile of papers
and a coffee. They have a coffee and look around, reaffirming
their faith in history. All the other old houses on the street,
including the matching twin to Barry and Joy's, have been
renovated inside and out. The matching twin is right next
door, but no one would recognize the resemblance. The twin
has vinyl siding and plastic bubbles on the roof and aluminum windows and a rear addition with sun-deck, hot tub and
shower. The guy who owns it put in urea formaldehyde insulation a few years ago and then had to rip it all out. Urea
formaldehyde was recommended by the government, but then
it was found to be poisonous. Ripping it out is a complicated
process that involves chainsawing the old siding and tongue
and groove shiplap off, stripping out the foam and bagging it,
sandblasting the studs and treating them with a chemical,
stuffing in fibreglass insulation, nailing on plywood and put-

ting on the new siding. Earlier this summer, I watched the whole process from the dining room window. Barry and Joy are lucky that they don't have enough money to make such significant improvements. The people from the historical society admire their good taste.

Living in town is very disorienting for me. I am paranoid about breaking something and Joy is a super housekeeper. I over-water the plants, of which there are dozens, hanging in every window. I worry about the dishes, the piano, the drum set, the records, the rugs. I am always advising the kids to be careful. At the same time, I am attracted to all the comforts. In the evenings while the inside of the house is cooling off, I sit in the back yard and read or have a beer and nod at the neighbours who are also out having a beer and nodding. Barry and Joy have a coffee maker, a colour TV with video, a stereo and tons of records, a washer and dryer and an electronic typewriter. Also the house is only a fifteen minute walk from the downtown. It is very pleasant to go out once or twice a week and watch a show and get mildly drunk and walk home in the cool dark.

Sometimes I am torn between the house and the farm. I am used to working at my sunny desk in view of the forest and I am not used to having a telephone or neighbours. I am used to doing a series of small necessary jobs like chopping wood and hauling water. I am also used to doing a number of big seasonal jobs like cutting hay, painting buildings and filling up potholes in the road. These things keep me fit. At Barry and Joy's, I have nothing to do except write and go out for a drink, a situation that only a fool would put himself into.

Barry and Joy's house is, however, perfect for my kids. They can stay with me there. They have outgrown the farm though they still think of it as the family home and have all kinds of tangled emotional connections with it. Victoria and Jennifer are both working so they have to live in town. They are addicted to morning showers, blow dryers, stereo, colour TV, electric lights, and telephones. Wesley can still live in the country where he keeps up a tangible residence. His trail bike is there when it isn't in the repair shop, and his collection of Marvel and Freak Bros. comics. His upstairs room is full and messy and looks recently slept in even when he hasn't been there for weeks. It is stocked with tent, sleeping bag, tarps, axe, etc., ready for the week-long camping trips to various lakes in the area where he and his friends fish, sleep, play cards, ride trail bikes, read Playboys and practise drinking. Jennifer's room is bare, and I have moved all my stuff into Victoria's room and packed all her stuff under the bed.

I once thought that I could keep the kids on the farm when they are with me, but I have had to change my ideas. Last winter, Jennifer and I had a major fight about this. We were all having burgers at the Camelot Cafe and I was enumerating the improvements I was going to make on the farm – namely a sundeck and a brick barbecue. Jennifer told me pointedly that she did not intend to spend another six months with me on the farm. She stated quite clearly that she "hated it there" and would make a deal to stay all year with her mother. I pointed out that her mother had plans to move south and besides living on the farm was very cheap and enabled me to save money for her education.

I was lucky that Alison was there. She pointed out that living in town was really quite cheap. "You spend almost $200 a month just on gas when you live out there," she said. "Also, if you lived in town, the kids could earn some of their own money. You can rent a two-bedroom place like mine for $400 a month. It's all very reasonable. The world isn't going crazy while you're out there chopping wood and listening to the CBC."

Jennifer snuggled up to Alison and put her head on her shoulder. I said I'd think about it. I didn't want to get into any financial argument with Alison. She knows more about money than I do. Besides, she was right and I subsequently revised my opinion and agreed to rent. Jen and Wes decided immediately on a highrise. They liked Alison's apartment. It has a pool and is only a fifteen minute walk from anywhere. However, a highrise is unlikely as pets are not allowed and

Jen has a cat. Also, their mother hasn't had any luck so far selling her house, so it is likely we will rent it from her when she moves and thus keep the money in the family, broken as it may be.

Jen and Wes have decided not to go with their mother. They will miss her but they want to graduate with their class. Also, things are more tense at their mother's place because she has a live-in girlfriend and the girlfriend has a daughter who is younger than Wes but taller and uses Jennifer's makeup without asking. I on the other hand lead a quiet bachelor's life. My sexual affairs are conducted with due formality. This is a surprise to me. When I was married, I always assumed that if I wasn't married I would fuck anything. Of course, when I was going out with Carol I was on the street at 5 AM fondling the door handles on her Volkswagen, but that was over a year ago and ended last spring when Victoria had a fight with her mother and came to live with me and Harvey.

This spring I got lucky again and Wes is with me. He had a fight over the mess in his room. Jennifer delivered him out to the farm. She told me that Wes was also accused of making smart remarks at my ex-wife's girlfriend's kid. Also, he is generally snide, sarcastic and smart-ass towards his mother. Jennifer figured this was all true but at the same time Wes was justified. "He's the only man in the place," she explained. "He won't let anyone else into the nest."

Wes was sad and lonely. He wanted to make up with his mother. He says he likes the girlfriend but the kid is too much to take. I tried to talk him into going back but not very enthusiastically. I had to make sure he felt welcome. Also, I was very glad to see him. I needed someone to look after. I was starting to feel lonely. It threw me off my routine but that was ok. Instead of getting up at 7 AM and making coffee and going to work on my book about the local poets, I had to drive him to school. Often I stayed in town to pick him up at three. I resumed my job routine, even though it was May. I hung around the office, public library and cafes. I got some writing done. I stopped dreaming at night. If I woke up, I could listen to him breathing or moving in the next room. I had somebody to wash clothes and dishes for. I didn't have to go to movies by myself, or drive into town in the afternoon to hit the bars. That can be a waste of money and driving home half drunk is not a good idea.

I wonder what will happen when the kids are gone. Victoria has already finished a year of Nursing at UBC. Jen graduates from high school this year. You can't just sit in a shack all day and write. You can't just be alone. Now that Donna has been transferred to Kamloops and Alison is going to Calgary, I have to face the prospect of another girlfriend. When I was married I would meet beautiful and/or interesting women and think it would be paradise to sleep with them. Having slept with a few, I can report that it's alright. There's something to being married, though, and having a certain understanding. There's something to be said for variety, but a new woman every year or so means a lot of work. There are the preliminary stages, where you sit for hours in the bar and tell your stories, and then go home and fuck. This is great, except that if you have work to do you are considerably distracted. Finally, you have to sort out a routine or go under. Someday maybe I'll go under but not now. This is the dangerous stage. Here you face sudden rejection or subjection. You begin to wonder if it's worth it. Jerking off looks more and more attractive. But if you go that way you could turn into a confirmed bachelor flossing your teeth three times a day and following people around when they go into your kitchen.

Not that I want a permanent relationship. It seems to me that there are certain things that I have to do on my own. I need to learn how to sort things out. I don't want to end up babbling to the guy next to me in the geriatric ward about what might have been. I don't want to be philosophizing when the enemy is coming across no man's land. Right now I am sorting out Alison and I don't need any distractions. She will be in my album and stories with Brenda, Donna, Carol and my ex-wife, and there will be a collection of letters that may or may not say things. However, Alison and I were very mature about our relationship. This time there will be loneliness with no question marks to make it either more poignant or bearable. There will be no tangible strings holding me to the past.

A few weeks ago Wes and I left Victoria alone to water the plants and cut the grass at Barry and Joy's. We went to Vancouver. First we visited White Rock so Wes could spend a few days with his grandmother who will soon be my ex-mother-in-law. This brought back all kinds of old feelings. I went to high school in White Rock. It was a quiet, dusty town then, or at least it seemed so to me. I felt I was really out in the country. Now that I have lived in the real country it seems quite busy. Marine Drive is a steady parade of hotrods and motorcycles. Vans with waterbeds in the back are pulled up to the beach and the rear doors are flung wide open and the stereos turned up and the bronzed young men perched on the roofs and doors invite the beautiful bikini-clad girls on the boardwalk to come in and make love. The Hell's Angels have moved in and bought up a few beach-front boarding houses. One of these houses used to belong to an aunt of my friend Art and we often went there to cut the grass for her and the place was full of quiet old men who watched the ocean for months and years. The park, which used to be half wild, is now full all summer long of families and their smoking barbecues. None of this seems unusual to the young people who as usual take life as it is and do not have to worry about what is better or worse but who just live. They can live with waterbeds and barbecues and nuclear weapons. I am to them what the old men in the boarding house were to me. They were failures. They knew all about it even if they weren't talking.

Meanwhile, up the hill from the beach, behind all the new condos and terraced beach houses where the young people sit in the sun at 9 AM and drink beer, the older people tend their gardens and worry about crows. The older people spent all their lives working, raising kids, driving around in cars, buying things and dumping their garbage everywhere, and now they are into growing flowers and vegetables. Unfortunately, the crows are unimpressed. They have eaten the garbage and they want the gardens too. They have sunrise rallies at 6 AM and wake up the citizens. They dive-bomb people they don't like. The seagulls, who are considered to be more picturesque than the crows, move away. Also, a dead whale was recently found on the beach. Greenpeace is having an information meeting at the old railway station. Autopsy reports will be circulated and local "indian experts" will give their opinion. The indians are experts on the past, when the world was clean and humans were dirty. It is unlikely, however, that they will say anything. What is there to say? Maybe the crows killed the whale. Maybe there is as much garbage in the ocean as there is on the land.

It was strange to stay overnight at my mother-in-law's place. I slept in my sister-in-law's old bedroom. On the dresser was a picture of one of my ex-wife's old girlfriends. My mother-in-law is puzzled by things but doesn't say anything. She looks after her grandchildren and worries about her daughter and even me. In the morning I got up early and went for a walk. I walked past the old high school. Inside there is a picture of our graduating class. My ex-wife is first on the right in the second row. I am third from the left in the third row. We were in love and her mother worked and sometimes we would go home after school and screw on the chesterfield and then do our homework. I walked past the house where we rented a basement suite for the summer we got married. She worked in a drugstore to make the tuition for Nursing school and I commuted to the docks in Vancouver. She cooked meals and worried about birth control and I took up smoking a pipe and thought about my career. This was marriage in the early Sixties.

I walked down the stairs to the ocean. In White Rock, some of the streets turn into pedestrian trails with stairs where it is really steep. These trails are carved out of blackberry vines. Down below, the ocean sparkles, so inviting even in a cool morning breeze that you want to drop into it. Of course, when you get right down to it it stinks. The town long ago outgrew its sewage treatment plant (where I applied for a job every summer and never got one) and took the only reasonable course of dumping shit straight into the bay. The beach is closed down once in a while by the health authorities and it is suicide to eat the crabs.

After White Rock, Wes and I stayed at my parents' place for a few days. My parents are confused about my wife and me but don't ask any questions. My ex-wife's picture is still on the wall. They are convinced we will get back together someday. Originally, they didn't want us to get married. They had nothing against my wife but just thought we should wait until I had a job and bankroll. Now they miss her. My mother is silent but my father makes it very clear that he expects me to get her back. I assure him that I am doing my best but he has met Carol and Alison and doesn't believe me. He thinks I am having a great time.

While we were at my parents' place, Wes and I went out and bought a motorcycle. I hadn't planned this, even though I do have some extra money due to the fact that Victoria got a summer job and will be able to pay her own fees. I acted in flagrant disregard of my depression mentality which assures me that I will lose my job soon, that the economy will collapse, that the dollar will go down, and that the town I live in will die. Harvey tells me not to worry. He says it is ok if the dollar goes down and interest goes up. When the dollar hits zero, it will not matter what interest you pay. There is something wrong with this argument but I don't know what it is. I didn't buy the motorcycle because I believed Harvey. I bought it because a motorcycle is a great substitute for sexual love. My friend Graham bought a Yamaha 650 when he and his wife split up a few years ago. Wes and I bought our motorcycle from another old friend, Ian, who bought it after he and his wife broke up. He is into a permanent relationship and doesn't need it anymore.

I'm glad I did it. Since we got back from Vancouver, I've already made two trips to Quesnel to help Alison pack up her house while her husband scouted up a place in Calgary. I can cruise at 110, flit in and out of the Winnebagos, pass the semi trucks on the steep hills. The air is sweet and rich with smells that people in cars cannot experience. The baking forest is pungent, or someone has just cut his or her hay. I can experience the camaraderie of the biker. It is mandatory to wave, even when you are negotiating a curve at impossible vectors. At the drive-in cafes, you can talk to the bikers in leather suits and cowboy boots. This is the only time you can see the faces of the female bikers which are usually interesting if not beautiful. Of course there are dangers too. You could easily get pasted to the back of a Winnebago. That last wave could be your last. Also, motorcycle riding is conducive to sexual fantasies of a rare poignancy, and the condition of a lover's nuts in the proximity of a vibrating steel gas tank is one of the not-so-subtle agonies of biking. Graham once told me that the gently rolling hills of the Cariboo are particularly bad for this. He says he has never made it past the Shell station at McLeese Lake without stopping to jerk off.

I'd rather have Alison than the motorcycle but I'd rather have the motorcycle than a new girlfriend. Probably when winter sets in I will change my mind. My father is very upset about the motorcycle. He is worried that I will give it to Victoria to use during the winter. Victoria is all for this plan. She loves her 175 but the 500 is much sexier and she could put on her leathers and cruise Vancouver between autopsies. Barry figures I should keep the bike until November so that he and I could go on a few runs to McBride or Fort St. James and maybe meet a couple of young women who have nourished a burning lust (mingled with respect) for us ever since they took Composition 103. This would be a nice break from Composition 103.

Barry hasn't seen the bike yet. During my holidays Alison sold her house and came down to surprise Wes and me in Vancouver. Alison and I decided to ride the bike up to visit Barry and Joy at their cabin. Unfortunately it rained, so we took the truck. However, Barry was enthusiastic. He uses his bike to negotiate the long, winding road from his cabin down the peninsula to Gibson's Landing. You don't have to wait in line to get your bike on the ferry and the fare is cheap. Since he is married, however, he doesn't use it much. He spends most of his summer holiday working on his cabin and trucking his kids to the lakes and beaches. This year, he cut down all the giant cedars around his cabin. The place looked like a logging operation, which made Alison and me feel at home. Now they have a clear view of Agamemnon Channel and can watch the Powell River ferry come and go. The ferry shakes the blue inlet and green hills and its whistle sets time for the people along the shore. The people along the shore live in the dream-world of summer holidays where time is meaningless. They wake up and have coffee and if it is nice they swim casually out and untie their boats from their moorings and go out fishing. Their cabins are full of used junk from city homes so they don't have to worry about spills and scuffs and they wear their old clothes around, jeans and shirts cut off at the knees or elbows. Barry and Joy dream of living in their cabin all year round, though the rain and isolation in winter would probably drive them nuts. They are going to build a new place just below the old one, then rip down the old one and expand the new one up into its place. This goes against Barry's depression mentality, but he is still into home building. With luck he will finish before he or his kids or his wife are ready to leave. With luck, vacation cabins made of cedar and white pine, with big windows and wood heaters, will still be marketable, and the people who live there all year round will refrain from smashing them up or burning them down. With even more luck, he will actually end up there, fishing, combing the beach for firewood, writing poems for the world and loving Joy. I'd prefer it if he'd stay in the north, but after a while it doesn't matter much anyway.

My home on the farm is as finished as it will ever be and my only problem now is spending enough time there. Maybe I will lose it too and have to find another, two wheels pounding the highway or some other dream. Romantic dreams can come true when the romance is out of them, safely in the past. In my album on my desk at the farm, Alison is in my house, on my motorcycle. She is standing on the porch of Barry's cabin, against a dark background of cedar. She is burning hay in the spring, pushing wood into the stove in the summer kitchen. She is picking berries and skiing too but that is after the album ends. She is a doctor in Calgary and I am at my desk staring out the window across the cut hay at the trees.

Making the World Safe.

In September the janitors and secretaries got mad and picketed the college. They were marching around with cardboard signs and beating on the roofs of cars that drove into the parking lot. They are all very quiet people, mostly older with families, but they never got paid much and were disgusted with the managers who represent the businessmen who represent the politicians who represent the public who own the college. The managers were always getting big wages, going on free trips, feeling up secretaries, throwing expensive parties and barfing on the cafeteria and washroom floors. Last year the secretaries and janitors joined one of the big pulp mill unions and this year they hit the streets.

Joining the big union was a good idea. As a result, they get $150 a week plus $50 per dependent for picketing. This amounts to half of what they made while working. Also, the pulp union gives them burning barrels and firewood and comes around with coffee, donuts, and a potty truck. The big guys from the mill like talking to the well-groomed executive secretaries and motherly ladies from the library. They act very gallantly, carrying signs for the ladies, and once in awhile they give a good demonstration of how to take care of a scab student or faculty member.

The managers announced in the media that the issue was

not merely salaries and job descriptions. The issue was, who runs the college, the secretaries or the public who own it? Democracy was the real issue. The philosophy of the managers is clearly that, if you have a big democracy, you should not have any little democracies inside it. Do soldiers elect their sergeants? Do public servants elect their manager? Obviously, the bigger the democracy the more genuine it is. For example, the government represents all the people, whereas little democracies like chambers of commerce, service clubs, city councils, political parties, corporations, motorcycle gangs and labour unions each in themselves represent only a few of the people. Since the managers were hired by the people appointed by the people hired by the government, they were obviously more democratic than the union reps elected by a bunch of secretaries and janitors.

On the other hand, the law says that little democracies are alright. Political parties, after all, are little democracies that help the big democracy to run more efficiently. Through the little democracies, people get to participate directly and learn first-hand the complex rules of democracy. They learn how to move motions, debate, vote, obey the will of the majority, and adjourn. Also, in the big democracy the line of authority along which the will of the people is conveyed to the people is a long one and it is well-known that sometimes the will of the people is shorted out before it gets to them. Even the Pope (who is not elected by all Catholics), on his recent visit to this country, praised the work of the little democracies (mainly Indian band councils and unions) in keeping the spirit of freedom alive. The Pope's opinions greatly encouraged the secretaries and janitors. The politicians and managers, however, were miffed. The general opinion was that the Pope wouldn't have made such a partisan statement if he was the Queen.

During the first days of the strike, the faculty did not cross the picket line. Of course, you don't get paid for staying home, but our contract protects us from loss of our jobs. The faculty felt sorry for the students, but one's professional duty clearly does not involve getting beat up. Besides, if the faculty someday struck or were locked out, they would need the un-qualified support of the secretaries and janitors. In labour terms, this is known as solidarity. In particular, faculty would not cross the line because of Thelma, who slaved in the xerox room and was always cheerful and willing to make fast copies in an emergency. So they stayed at home worrying about their paycheques, pensions and mortgages, and hoping that the strike would end. They read books, listened for news on the radio, and tried to keep their families calm in the face of a $100 (gross) daily loss.

The managers, as a result, had nothing to manage but two thousand confused or angry students. The college was not ful-filling its public mandate. Some of the managers were told to teach classes but this was a disaster. There was an explosion in the chemistry lab. Though the management had received dozens of memos on the subject over the years, one of them had forgotten that the gas jets had been installed improperly and were "on" when they said "off." Another manager could not do the grade 12 algebra refresher. Some classes were devoted entirely to complaints about absent faculty and in others students were given application forms for correspond-ence courses. Students walked out of classes or asked angry questions. The managers got angry. When you are fighting for democracy you do not expect to be criticized. Soon the fight with the secretaries and janitors was forgotten, and the managers began to blame the whole mess on faculty.

This was hard. Faculty did not want to make the managers angry. Faculty are all very quiet and nice, mostly older people with families. They are members of Lions and Elks. They get paid fairly well and so can afford mortgages, car payments, and braces for the teeth of their well-washed, groomed, and bred sons and daughters. Their homes are neat and tastefully furnished and usually there is a motor home, camper, or trail-er in the driveway. They have an investment in society. Con-sequently they were scared when the managers threatened in public to cancel their courses if they didn't come to work.

Even the vague prospect of unemployment is a major threat

to my colleagues. Unemployment would destroy a lot of careful planning. It would mean the end of house and car payments, beautiful teeth and pensions. This last consideration is particularly important. When you talk about pensions, you are talking about the hearts of my colleagues. Pensions are the main subject of discussion in the staff lounge. A good deal of time goes into figuring out pensions – almost as much as goes into preparing lectures and marking papers. For my colleagues, pensions represent all of their hopes for the future. All of their insecurities regarding old age, joblessness, sickness and loneliness are soothed by the existence of pensions. Because of their pensions, my colleagues will be able to put on soft hats and T-shirts with messages on them, and drive their motor homes, trailers and campers all over the continent. They will get the best of medical attention. They will remain important to their children and never be a burden to anyone. They will regain their lost youth. They will travel, make love, and write poetry. They will be free.

There is of course the question of how appropriate this dependence on pensions is. Will my colleagues really be able to do what they hope to do, with or without their pensions? Many young people are skeptical about this, but what do they know? Young people have trouble conceiving of geriatrics taking off their clothes and making love. They prefer sports cars to motor homes. Perhaps my colleagues, all of them trained in the great thoughts of great men and women, very few of whom had pensions or motor homes, should've found a less worldly faith. Perhaps not.

I myself had no pension until a year ago. During my first twelve years at the college, I preferred to hang on to my youthful idealism. However, in all those years I published only about twenty poems and, although one or two of them are brilliant, my genius remains unrecognized. Also, my hair is turning grey. My skin is wrinkled. I have to get up in the middle of the night to pee. One night at the bar, Barry and I were discussing these matters. It disturbed us that we'd made it past the ten-year mark where the college matches your pension contributions. But we had no contributions to match. We got quite worked up about this. We decided that it is better to have something than nothing. We went in and signed up.

Of course, we will never put in the 30-35 years requisite to the collection of full benefits. Pensions are a tricky consideration. What you do is accumulate fifty or sixty thousand dollars in a special bank account. The bank in turn promises to pay you a regular wage after the age of sixty-five. The size of this wage depends on how many years you have put in, whether your employer has also made a contribution, and how high your wages are during your last five years of employment. You are gambling that you will work steadily for thirty-five years and then live for ten or more years past retirement. If you do, you will get back what you put in or more. The bank is gambling that you will break one of the rules and never reach full benefits. Either that or you will croak on your last day of work. If you do that, the bank gets most of your money.

All of this is further complicated by inflation. In order to keep your money safe over a long period of time, and pay itself for taking care of it, banks loan this money. Mainly, they loan it to government. The government is the only organization that has enough credit to borrow this much money. It has the credit because it prints the money. When you represent all of the people then you are entrusted with really vital responsibilities like conducting war, hanging people, and printing money. Government borrows your pension money and then leaves most of it in the bank and orders the bank to loan it to businessmen who use it to stimulate the economy. The system is perfect. People with pensions feel secure, because if you can't trust the government who can you trust? Businessmen get to play around with other people's money and stimulate the economy, and if businessmen can't stimulate the economy then who can? The banks get to collect lots of interest without any risk. The politicians get to decide to let other people decide. Even if the businessmen fail to stimulate the economy, no one really loses. The government prints more money to pay the pension funds with interest. Of course, inflation results from printing money, but inflation is a long-term consideration. No one worries much about it except those who are close to collecting a pension or already collecting it, and everyone knows that these people are old and out of touch if not senile.

Politics also affects the pensions. Recently, it seems, the bankers made a mistake and loaned pension money to governments in other countries. There was a lot of leftover pension money that the government in this country did not want. The businessmen, of course, wanted it, and the banks had to invest it somewhere in order to collect interest. Consequently, the bankers, businessmen, politicians and managers got together and decided it would be ok to lend pension money to friendly foreign governments. The economies of these foreign countries would be stimulated and this would make the world safe for free enterprise and democracy. Democracy would be seen to be putting its money where its mouth is. The system would spread around the world and communism would be fucked.

Unfortunately, the plan failed. It seems that South Americans and Africans are either lazy or crazy. In the old days it was assumed that this was caused by the sun but now we know that it is due to communism. At present, these other countries owe the pensioners a lot of money. They tried printing it, but the banks didn't want their money; they had enough of a problem with the money in the country. Rumour now is that these countries will never be able to pay off their loans. Sometimes it takes a very brutal dictatorship to ensure that the mere interest is paid. If it is not paid then the government of this country has to print more money to loan the banks so they do not collapse. Inflation increases. However, the peasants in foreign countries do not understand the importance of this. They do not want to live in slavery so that the pensioners in this country will get to drive their motor homes. They do not understand the importance of motor homes. They tend to go for communism, which tells them they have been ripped off by the banks and businessmen of this country. They have to be taught that a deal is a deal. This creates anxiety for the pensioners. They do not want to have to kill people in order to get their pension money back, though everyone admits that slavery and even death are preferable to communism.

A funny thing happens when people's backs are driven against the wall, when they are threatened or when the contradictions of their situation are too much to understand. Some of them collapse and will do anything they are told. Others get stubborn. One of the rules of sound management is not to let either of these things happen. Another equally ancient rule, however, in tricky situations, is to divide and conquer. The managers were in a tricky situation and saw their chance. When they started cancelling courses, faculty started crossing the picket line. Ultimately, almost half of them crossed. It was a rout. Even Thelma couldn't stop them. If she stood in front of their Volvos and Rabbits they would say things like "I have to eat," or "I owe it to my students," or "I've only got four years left," or they would give her an analysis of the British Coal Strike of 1979 and the Air Traffic Controllers Strike of 1980 as examples of the futility of unionism at the present time. Thelma would have to say "What about me?" or "Fuck you" and let them go in.

The other half of the faculty, however, got angry. Their anxieties had been played upon once too often. Thoughts of crooked teeth, mortgages, pensions and motor homes were consumed by anger. They became human once again, some for the first time since childhood. Their eyes flashed. They spoke with feeling. They were not afraid. Some who went in during the rout came shamefacedly back out and were met with great rejoicing and gestures of comradeship around the burning barrels. Then they all began turning up at the picket lines early in the morning to walk with the secretaries and janitors. The pulp union produced more coffee. People came around with folders and pamphlets about peasants in South America and Africa. When the managers or scabbing colleagues drove in, they gave them the finger or kicked at their fenders. They sang inspirational songs and talked tactics.

Most of the discussion around the burning barrels concerned who was going in and who wasn't, or who had gone in and come out or come out and gone in. "Charlie!" you'd say. "Wasn't he on the executive last year?" or "Didn't we just get him an arbitration settlement on that overload he had last semester?" Someone would explain that the Dean had gotten to him, possible rejection of a proposed leave or cancellation of a favourite course. Or else Charlie's wife had gotten to him, crying all through the afternoon, ashamed to go shopping with her friends, shivering at night so that Charlie had to put her in a hot bath for an hour. Anyway, Charlie was in, and Bill, who knew more about the British Coal Strike than was good for him.

Meanwhile, the union executives would stroll around and tell you about the latest letter of support from colleagues from the south or the latest unfair labour practise charge launched against management. For example, the English Department, which Barry and I belonged to, all the members of which were proudly supporting the picket line, was suing for libel because the Dean had said, in the local paper, that correspondence courses were better than regular ones and anyway certain English teachers weren't very good. Barry would tell the secretaries that his chances of becoming poet laureate of England were blown all to ratshit by the Dean's rash statement, and that $100,000 wouldn't be a fair settlement though he'd take it if he had to.

Around noon, everyone would drift home, leaving the secretaries and janitors alone, sitting around the burning barrels reading bad novels. Barry and I would go to the cafe for a soup. For an hour, we would discuss finances and drink as much coffee as the waitress would give us. Barry would consider the merits of pulling his $5,000 in registered retirement savings, money he was saving for his next sabbatical leave. He was planning to go to Greece to write poetry. His wife Joy was planning to go to university to study Criminology. Either way, it was going to cost. I was selling things: my rototiller, my mimeograph, my trail bike. I was looking around for a contractor to log some timber off my farm. Privately we admitted to one another that we wanted the strike to last. The emotional rush of registration had died. We were used to going for a soup at noon and a beer in the evening. I said I would stay out until hell freezes over if need be. Barry said he would stay out even longer. He wished he was back in his cabin at Sechelt. "What's the use of being off work in this place? I can't even ride the motorcycle any more. Soon it'll be snowing."

We watched our colleagues. As time passed, it got more and more like war, with the real advantage that nobody got killed. We had always considered most of the faculty to be a bunch of amiable simpletons. For one thing, they didn't like the union that much and were always whining about professionalism. We'd given up on that years ago. We saw how the managers were taking over. There were computers everywhere. People who went to the Phillipines for Japanese Management seminars were not impressed with our publication lists. They thought that poetry was shit. Two years ago, Barry had had his Creative Writing course cancelled on him, and last year he was laid off and came back only by virtue of a lot of lobbying and an arbitration threat. We knew the managers were out to get us. As Barry said, "Habeas corpus transvestus under the N 13," the Pope's own words, which can be roughly translated as "You can't scare me, I'm stickin' to the union."

Consequently, the strike was easier for us than it was for most of our colleagues. We had drawn that line. The managers were assholes, fuckfaces, perverts and shit-eaters. It was plain as the nose on your face. Most of the other faculty were still trying to be reasonable. What they discovered was that reasonableness has limits. The people who ran Auschwitz were reasonable. They didn't hate the Jewish people. They just did what they were told. The fanatics who hated the Jewish people knew better than to kill them themselves. If you want any kind of work done you get reasonable people to do it for you. They will do a good job. They will remember to keep clear records and pry out the gold teeth before the corpses are burnt. Once you start them off, they will continue the work with due attention to detail just as if they were mowing the lawn or paying bills.

For a while, our executive stood back to see what would happen. They were nervous. They had to represent the majority and it was hard to say if the majority were in or out. The managers provided the local paper with one set of figures, and the union provided a different set. We took it day by day. We had lots of meetings in a downtown hotel. There were no agendas. Some information (usually disappointing) was provided concerning negotiations between the secretaries and the managers. Then there were long speeches about whether the secretaries had good leadership, what was going to happen in two months when our own contract was up, etc. Those who crossed the line discussed the British Coal Strike and the futility of radical unionism, and those who didn't cross said that the strike would've ended weeks ago if we'd all stood firm. This resulted in further speeches by those who went in, about the sufferings of students who were losing a year, which led to speeches about faculty who thought they were being professionals by bending over so that management could shine a light up their assholes. This led to speeches about radicals and leftists which led to speeches about scabs and skunks until finally someone moved to adjourn and everyone drifted, talking and arguing, to the bar.

During one of these meetings I got depressed. It seemed to me that we were drifting. I scribbled a motion to the effect that we fine everyone who was working $100. I thought about it and changed it to $200. I figured that this would bring some faculty back out and provide a fund for those of us who were out. When I proposed my motion, Barry seconded it and then moved to amend it to $300. I seconded his amendment. Then one of the scabs moved that we table the motion for further study. This confused a lot of people; they weren't sure what was happening. The President explained that the motion could be taken off the table at some future meeting by a majority vote. Someone thought that taking it off the table meant throwing it in the garbage. Even though they agreed that it was garbage, they thought it was unfair to me and Barry to chuck it out without a vote. The President explained that taking it off the table meant voting on it. The motion to table was then seconded. There were cries of "question, question" and the President asked for a vote. Someone objected that the people with questions should be allowed to ask them. The President explained that to call the question meant to vote. We voted, and the motion to table was lost. Then the President asked if there was any discussion of the main motion. He was reminded that Barry's amendment had to be voted on first. The President then ruled that Barry's amendment was friendly since I had seconded it. Thus, it became part of the main motion. Someone moved to amend the main motion to read $150 rather than $300 on the grounds that $300 was too high. The President asked me and Barry if we thought this was a friendly amendment and we agreed that it was friendlier than anything we'd heard so far. The President called for any discussion and the secretary put up his hand and said that, according to our Constitution (which he had been busy reading), all motions concerning fines, levies, dues or assessments required a two-week notice and a two-thirds majority. The President sat down heavily in his chair. Then he asked me if I intended to give notice of my motion. I said I was so doing.

In the ensuing days, Barry and I were heroes to those on the picket line. Our colleagues clapped us on the shoulders. The daycare women in particular, who were another department to stay out en masse, were very encouraged. The head of that department, Connie, told us that she was very heartened by our motion. "We have to do it," she said. "If we don't we'll be screwed if we have to go on strike in December."

"Jesus," said Barry later on. "She's pretty nice."

"Picket lines make me horny," I said.

Barry agreed.

On the other hand, the faculty who were working hated us. They told us they would quit any union that forced them to compromise their professional ethics. We reminded them of the vote to support the secretaries and janitors, and the strike/lockout clause in our own contract. "Your ethics are shit," we said. "Go in and suck ass," we jeered. "Fucking scabs." Our union executive took us aside. "You guys are dividing the union," they said. We pointed out that we were divided. Half of us were in making money, and the other half were out, losing it. "That's nothing," said the executive, "to what would happen if your motion is voted down. That could demoralize people and drive them all in."

We admitted that this was a serious consideration. Some careful lobbying was obviously in order. We went to see Connie. She went to the executive and they agreed to get our lawyers up to advise us on the legality of my motion, and to make any suggestions regarding fines or levies. Our lawyer duly arrived at the meeting when the vote was to be taken. He is a young Jewish guy with an Afro haircut. He is very good at winning arbitrations. Of course he has a deep attachment to the union movement, so you have to disregard most of what he says. He made a great speech. He told us that he admired those of us who had stayed out. He exhorted the others to reconsider their actions.

He reminded us of our glorious history of arbitration awards, and the piles of money that the managers had paid out for wrongful dismissal, failure to negotiate technological change, etc. He praised our collective agreement, pointed out that it guaranteed our professional as well as our monetary interests. He said that my motion was probably illegal. He referred to three precedents. The main problem, it seemed, was that we were not a closed shop. "What's a closed shop?" I asked Connie. She didn't know. Our lawyer then said that he had examples of special assessment clauses that could go in our constitution and work as well as any fine. He advised us to go that route.

The President then got up and said that he would, accordingly, rule my motion out of order. Then someone moved that my motion be rejected. I seconded the motion but the secretary said that you can't move a motion to reject a motion. He recommended that we all simply vote against my motion. My motion was unanimously defeated. I volunteered to tear it up and piss on it, but the President thought that it had been dealt with to everyone's satisfaction.

Later that evening, Connie, Barry and I and the executive met with our lawyer in the bar. We discussed the possibility of a special assessment of 20 percent on all working faculty "to enable the union to continue in times of strike or lock-out." The President explained that, though he fully agreed with such a motion in principle, he didn't want to put it to the membership without due preparation. He talked ominously about a decertification movement starting inside the college, backed by the managers. "This motion," he said, "could turn a lot of people against us." "If they tried that," said our lawyer, his eyes flashing, "we could get an injunction." We agreed to let the executive handle the timing of the motion, so long as they didn't put it off for too long. We pointed out that we were going broke. We agreed to start lobbying right away.

The discussion was over. People finished their drinks and got up. Barry and I figured on asking Connie to come to the lounge for a drink, but before we got the chance she stood up and headed off with our lawyer.

"Shit," said Barry.

"Maybe they went up to his room to read Marx," I said.

"They're going to a meeting of the contract committee," said the President, significantly. "Maybe you remember we are also into negotiations at the present time. Maybe you'd like to sit in and keep your eye on her. Actually we could use a couple more people on that committee."

"No thanks," I said.

"I'm going home," said Barry.

"How long is the contract meeting?" I asked.

"Our lawyer has to be at the airport in an hour," said the

President. "I'm taking him there myself. Any more questions?"

"No," I said.

The President rushed off to the contract meeting. Barry went home. I sat around for an hour to see if Connie would come back into the bar but she didn't.

Who Has Seen the Teacher?

Today is the first day of spring semester and I have a cold. I get a lot of colds. One theory is that job and life pressures generate psychosomatic symptoms like colds, backaches, insomnia and migraines. This can hit particularly hard in middle age when you are usually locked into your job and life. You can't quit your job because the chances of getting another one are slim and your kids depend on you for nourishment. You are halfway through your mortgage and halfway to your pension. Also, you are beginning to recognize certain limitations. You will not get to Hollywood and fuck Jane Fonda.

Another theory is that people get sick in an arbitrary fashion due to micro-organisms, accidents and stupidity. This is not a particularly interesting perspective, unless stupidity can be said to include the phenomena described in the first theory.

Fortunately for me, my kids are still down in Victoria visiting their mother. They went down for New Year's. I can wander around the house moaning until 3 AM without waking anyone up. I wish I could be alone for a few more days and get rid of the cold and clean up the house, but the kids are coming home in two days and anyway I am not very motivated. Last night I turned on the TV and watched a movie about a guy who blew up roller-coasters.

Presently, I am at the office in a brief break between meetings and a two-hour bout on the registration desk in the gym. I am waiting for Milton to show up. Milton is one of my favourite students. Last semester he took the Survey of World Literature course from me. This semester, he wants to take my Canadian Literature course. I have been trying to talk him out of this move, so far unsuccessfully.

Milton is 5 foot 10, 200 pounds, 19 years old, and Chinese. He has a round face with round eyes peering through round glasses. His hair is jet black and stands straight up and has a permanent part down the middle that looks like it was made by a bullet. Milton wears a white shirt and jeans with big cuffs, white socks and black shoes with thick rubber soles. He talks very fast and is fluent though his spelling when he writes is terrible. He is saving for a word-check program for his computer and I hope he gets it soon. He says he was born in Canada but his parents had just arrived here then and still speak only Cantonese, and he learned English by watching TV for eight hours every day. When he writes essays he compares Hamlet to Charlie Brown, Sherlock Holmes to Kojak and Hedda Gabbler to Joan Collins in *Dynasty*. He says he is still addicted to TV but has got it down to about four hours since he got the computer.

Milton gets along well with Barry, who has learned a lot from Milton about the Chinese. For example, Chinese people don't have hair on their chests. Also, they never go to bars. They prefer to drink at home, where they drink mostly whisky. Chinese people mature more rapidly than Europeans. Milton has been 5 foot 10 and 200 pounds ever since he was 11. In high school he went to all the X-rated movies and strip-shows in town. He just sat there looking big and inscrutable and no one ever asked him for ID. Then he told his friends all about what he saw. Last semester, when we got to Lawrence in World Literature, Milton told the class the plot of *Lady Chatterly's Lover*. He didn't have the story quite right but it had a lot of action. He had the idea that Lady Chatterly's lover bumholed her all the time instead of fucking her in the usual way and this was why she loved him so much. Some of the students tried to pretend that they weren't interested.

Milton brought in his grade 9 student card to show us what he looked like in the old days. He did look the same. "It looks like you were even shaving then," said Barry. "Actually," said Milton, "I've never shaved in my life. I look like I do, but it doesn't grow out. It just stays like that."

Milton is very conservative. He says we are the first left wingers he's ever known. He gets his politics from his father, who owns a grocery store, hates unions and says that the only downtown renewal we need here is to shoot all the bums. He is in the Business Program. He runs his own business selling diet pills, but you can't legally call them diet pills. They are diet supplements. Each pill contains vegetables, meat and cereals, all magically released when you drink a glass of water with the pill. The business is a pyramid, so Milton doesn't actually sell the pills. This is probably a good thing, because Milton doesn't use the pills himself except to snack on between meals. This is how he understands the word "supplement." He is always popping one in his mouth. What Milton does is hire students to sell the pills. Each student buys a kit for $50. Milton gets 10 percent. The kit has two bottles of pills, ten little cans of samples and lots of brochures and testimonials. Milton gets 10 percent of all sales. He keeps his supplies in the back of his father's store and lumbers around town sucking on pills and making deliveries.

Also, Milton belongs to Conservative Youth. Barry tells him he might as well give up on politics. "They'll never trust you," says Barry. "You need a new hairdresser. You need polyester slacks and a tie. You shouldn't be taking literature courses. Face it, Milton. You're a mutant. We're your only friends."

However, Milton is serious about politics. He wants to help us. He is convinced that the college suffers from bad management. We are convinced of this too, but often bad management is better than good management, if you know what I mean.

Last semester, Milton got angry about a Math course that he took. He found out that he couldn't get any university credit for it. He went to the local MLA's office and retailed all the gossip about administration that he'd picked up in our office. He told the MLA's executive assistant that he had some complaints about the college. He told her about the Math course. He told her how certain administrators had wrecked a motel room during a think tank. Apparently, they tried to flush a golf cart down the toilet. He demanded to know how much it had cost to repair the damage. He told her that certain administrators spent most of their time working for companies run by Board members. He told her how the purchasing agent fucked the president of the Women's Athletic Club and the Dean of Behavioral Sciences felt up a student during hypnosis sessions designed to increase her power of concentration.

The MLA's assistant wrote all this down, but the only result was that Barry and I got a phone call from the Dean. He was very angry but so were we. We told him that the executive assistant had told Milton that all English instructors were homos and that the purchasing agent couldn't get it up anyway. We told the Dean to investigate these complaints as we were thinking of getting a lawyer and Milton was ready to testify on our behalf.

I enjoy having Milton around but I don't really want him to take my Canadian Literature course. Milton is from another culture and besides he is a businessman. Canadian Literature is, on the whole, embarrassing. On the whole, it can only be studied as a career or patriotic duty. Most of it was written to form. Take Grove, for example. He is the first writer we study this semester. Could I teach Grove to Milton? Grove is an example of the Prairie Novel that is a distinctive type in Canadian Literature. It is so distinctive that when you see a TV short based on a prairie novel you instantly know it for what it is and turn it off. All prairie novels work the same way:

Husband and wife work the land.

Wife gets fed up and sleeps with hired hand.

Children are used by their father like domestic animals, beasts of burden.

And by their mother to fulfill her thwarted cultural ambitions.

And they go to the city and can't really play the cornet.

Not as good as the black individual down the street.

Meanwhile, the land fights this twisted human intrusion. The fields are ploughed to powder to soak up winter snow and spring rain.

And the wind blows the fields away again.

And in summer the farmer scrapes over the roof of his house, over the bottom of his well. Prepares the land again to net the wind.

Some critics see in this an archetype of what happens in an economic system grounded upon exploitation and energized by expansion, a system that destroys the commonality of language and fattens the priests of capital on the divine substance of humanity.

Most readers see a bunch of stupid people doing stupid things.

The dust jackets, however, tell a different story. According to them, prairie novels are laced with lusty humour, touched by compassion, and uncompromisingly honest. They are entertaining and enjoyable incursions into time and the true nature of Canadian character. They are stories one might expect from an author who has won the Leacock Award for Humour and the Governor General's Award and the Nobel Prize. They contain prose that rings with the authentic click and clatter of combines and the farting of horses, prose that is clear, colourful, unpretentious, forceful, with an undercurrent of sincerity and compassion. They tell stories that blow the lid off life in a prairie town and shove it up your asshole.

The trouble is that the history of the prairies has a special attraction for middle-class white Canadian writers who don't know their assholes from gopher holes but who do know what the other white writers who hand out Canada Council grants are going to like. For example, Canadian Literature is full of stories and poems based on the story of Dumontriel and those who sought his leadership. Chief Running Water. Chief Septik Tank. Chief Airtight Heater. He died at the hands of a stray bullet. Middle-class white Canadian writers love all this because it was one of the few great rebellions in our history and middle-class people love rebellions. They are always "nice" or "responsible" on the surface and prefer consultation over confrontation. But underneath they dream of anarchy, retribution, destruction and the end of everything, especially their jobs.

I wonder what Louis Riel would think of all this. Probably be glad his name is in print, at any price. He was crazy. The strain of fighting in the resistance was too much. He didn't have the technique. They say, though, that his friend Gabriel Dumont did. He knew when you could talk to people and when you just had to take your gun and blow their fucking heads off.

RIEL: I had a dream last night.

DUMONT: I never dream. Sometimes Madelaine tells me about her dreams. She loves talking about them. She asks me, Gab, tell me about your dreams.

RIEL: I saw a man with the head of a buffalo. He asked me, where are my brothers? I couldn't answer. Then he showed me a place in the prairie and thousands of buffalo were there. They ran into that place and disappeared!

DUMONT: I heard of that place. The indians say the buffalo disappeared into a hole there.

RIEL: Is there such a place?

(Dumont points to the bore of his rifle.)

The buffalo man is the Métis. We are half and half, like him, and we live off the buffalo. We are all brothers.

DUMONT: Louis, I wish that I had your gift of prophecy. How do you feel?

RIEL: Weak, my friend. The visions come over me, day and night. The spirits are crying out to me.

DUMONT: Have some tea. Let me tell you a story my mother used to tell me. Gab, she would say, let me tell you why the buffalo love the Métis. What? I would ask. We kill them! You fool! she would say. They let us kill them. Why do you think it's so easy? I'll tell you why. Before the Métis came with their big rifles, the buffalo were in trouble. One year they would walk from Red River to the mountains, eating all the grass and leaving great piles of "night soil" behind. The next year they would eat from the mountains back to Red River. Each year they manured the land, each year the grass grew higher, each year there were more buffalo. Finally, they were shoulder to shoulder, over all the prairie. They couldn't move any more! It was eat and shit, shit and eat. They were almost smothered! Then the Métis came. You know what great appetites we have. We killed the buffalo. The buffalo could move again. The grass shrank back. The shit dried up. Now they were happy. So every year the buffalo let us kill as many of them as we want.

RIEL: That story means that we, the Métis, are right. Only the buffalo can live on the prairie, and only the Métis are smart enough to live on the buffalo.

DUMONT: My father used to say that story was bullshit.

This little drama would never sell to the Canada Council. It needs a setting, for the essence of prairie fiction is its peculiar locale which, intertwining with elements of plot and character, forms a symbolism stark and powerful. For what is prairie but a manifestation of the levelling force of fate, which would eternally remind us that even our most permanent achievements of railway, road and townsite are products of tight-ass Pythagorean abstraction, mental forces that are finally about as powerful as a fart in a windstorm?

"He used to say it was bullshit," said Dumont, looking deeply into the embers of his *fire*.

"In one sense, yes," said Riel, his black locks streaming in the *wind*.

As he spoke, the false fronts of a nearby town crashed down under the relentless pressure of the *wind*.

"Shit," said the mayor.

"This isn't working," said John A. Macdonald. "I ask for

prairie symbolism, and I get shit." He summoned Andy Sukiyaki, one of Canada's great ethnic poets, to his office. "Andy," he said expansively, "I want a Canada stretching from sea to sea. Nor am I such a dotard as to believe that such an enterprise can succeed on the basis of mere materialism. The work of Walsh, of Van Horne, of Fraser and Palliser, of" and here Macdonald leered broadly "the oldest profession, is all very well. But where are the heroines and heroes, the legends that will inspire the people to fill these institutions with life?"

"Gee Klise," said Sukiyaki. "All time slame ting."

But Macdonald reached across his desk and handed him a grant application form. It was him or Barry McKinnski or (even worse) the great west-coast ethnic poet Harvey Chometskiski. So he signed and faced RIELITY!

This is the fate of most Canadian writers. The one obvious exception is Malcolm Lowry, but can he be said to be Canadian? Why not? If, say, Grove can be, so can Lowry. Or is the basic qualification really nothing more or less than complicity with the status quo, confusion, and well-deserved failure?

I'm presently reading a biography of Lowry. He's been a hero of mine since I was in first-year university and had to read *Under the Volcano*. I learned then that he lived at Dollarton. Deep Cove, just past Dollarton, was always one of my favourite places and when I was a kid on Main Street in Vancouver, I often rode my bicycle across town, over the old bridge with the centre span that went up and down, through the indian reservation, past Dollarton and around Deep Cove. Who knows – maybe I even passed Lowry on the road while I cranked my rusty CCM. I wouldn't have looked up because looking up made it harder to crank. Judging by what I read, he wouldn't have looked up either. He would've been calculating the probability of getting a drink in the near future. I was usually with my friend George who suffered horribly from asthma. I never knew if George was going to make it but he was always game. Sometimes I had my sister with me. I had to wait for her on the hills but I enjoyed buying her a pop at the roadside grocery store at Dollarton. Later, when I was at university, I heard that they built a park at Dollarton and there was some kind of memorial to Lowry there but I never went over to check it out. I tried hard to read *Volcano* but couldn't get into it. Years later I read all the other stuff and it was great, especially the stories about Dollarton.

I don't teach Lowry in Canadian Literature. Lowry is hard to understand, which is great but not when you have to teach him. Or rather, not when you have to teach him by objectives, which is how all teaching at our college is presently done. If you have to teach by objectives, you are more inclined to teach prairie novels. This is why Grove is on the curriculum and likely to stay there forever. His grammar is good. His message is very clear. Unfortunately, the quality of his work is very clear too, but when you teach by objectives quality is not an important consideration. That is the concern of literary critics and the sooner they get their shit together and decide what is good and what isn't and why, the better. The theory of objectives presumes that students should find the world in order and be a part of it. When Dick and Jane go to the dentist he doesn't give them a blow job and is not a former member of the SS. The fact that any real Dick and Jane are (statistically) quite likely to have encountered certain highly abnormal human beings is a problem for psychiatrists, social workers and the RCMP. They are supposed to standardize life so it is safe, and the sooner they get their shit together and do it the better. Meanwhile, we in the school system do the best we can.

Objectives are very popular in the schools right now and are thought by some to be the only way that teachers can rationalize their existence to the politicians and thus avoid any future pay cuts. Actually, in the outside world, objectives are already very déclassé, and Japanese Management is the new thing. Schools, however, are always twenty years behind the times and teachers are old enough to be indulgent. Besides, Japanese Management is not for us. We remember the old war movies, that voice out of the jungle darkness after

Sarge has left the foxhole: "Hey Yankee. We have your friend. Hear him scream!" We remember footage of Pearl Harbour, Hong Kong and concentration camps in the Philippines. We prefer good old American ingenuity, which as everyone knows is based on individualism and democracy instead of regimentation and fascism.

Objectives have to be numerical, or how can you verify that they have been achieved? For example, you can't say, "The student will learn to write." You have to say, "The student will learn to identify and correct misplaced modifiers (comma faults, spelling errors, etc.) in 9 out of 10 samples." Obviously, you can't test for these things by merely asking students to write. Indeed, if you teach writing by objectives you have to avoid writing as much as possible. You have to use short answer and multiple-choice tests. The trouble with writing is that it introduces the element of choice. When writing a paragraph or essay, the student may avoid certain problems with spelling etc. by writing like Hemingway. Also, when a student writes he or she could decide that there are more important considerations than spelling and misplaced modifiers. The student could get involved, excited, inspired and say something that has never been said before. The student could then expect to be judged on this unquantifiable element. This would screw up the whole system of objectives.

Milton, for example, is usually inclined to express himself on various issues when he writes. He is always in a hurry to find out what I think about what he thinks. He will argue endlessly over Hamlet, whether he is heroic or not. He is always surprised when I tell him that he got a "P" because there are twenty spelling errors on every page. He is momentarily embarrassed for me when I mention it. He doesn't understand that, no matter how great his ideas, if he fails to improve his spelling he could be in college for the rest of his life. Luckily for him, he always gets "A"s in all his other courses. In Economics he even won a Texas mickey. Each member of the class was given ten thousand hypothetical dollars to invest in the Toronto Stock Exchange. You had to study the reports in the *Globe and Mail* and manage your investment. By the end of the semester, Milton doubled his money. His closest competitor made half as much. The teacher lost $1,000.

Another thing about Milton is that he always wants to know what I think about the latest bestsellers. Of course he never reads them himself, but he sees the movies and the reviews in *Time*. I tell him that bestsellers are crap. No great writer will write the latest bestseller. If you are a great writer, you are a member of the resistance. You are an enemy of the state. You don't just sit under the trees all day and smell the flowers. You also pay the price for sitting under the trees. Society doesn't necessarily like to see people sitting under trees. On the other hand, society is always watching to see if sitting under the trees is becoming groovy. If it is, then the resistance suddenly becomes culture. Society stops hanging people who sit under trees and starts sitting under trees itself. Long hair is in and rhyme is out. Trees become scarce. Flowers are at a premium. Sunsets play to packed houses. Meanwhile, millions of teenagers and a few artists lose their innocence and have little if anything to replace it with. The writer, if he or she survives, moves on. Milton thinks this is all very colourful but he still figures that Barry and I should write stories like Arthur Hailey.

Maybe he's right. I wouldn't want to be like Lowry. His life was rough. He stepped into the front lines. They weren't invisible to him, they were all over the landscape. The fascists didn't blow him away as he feared but the strain of waiting for it to come finally got to him. They burned down his shack. They closed the liquor stores on Sundays. They threw him in jail. They dried him out. They considered lobotomy. Lowry was willing to agree. He knew it was the only way to make everyone happy. After all, that was the moral of all his stories.

Grove, on the other hand, decided to lie his way out. This is a slower form of lobotomy and infinitely more painful, especially for others. He decided that a novelist was someone who wrote in the third person about heroes working out moral dilemmas against the backdrop of realistic descriptions of an indifferent universe. Har, har. Very professional. Of course, if professionals were honest there would still be forests, the news would be accurate and the poor would be cared for. Teachers would write poems and Canadian Literature would not be so embarrassing. If Grove had really believed this, he wouldn't have hidden his former life, he would've written it up. Milton would've loved it. What does Milton care about prairie farmers who work all day and never fuck someone in the ass or something interesting like that? Obviously, such a character has no imagination and his moral dilemmas are not worth thinking about. Grove had a great life, full of fear, despair, betrayal, adultery and other things that everyone can understand. But he never told it. He never said anything about what he really knew, which is all Lowry ever did on earth and all I want to do. Whenever possible.

When the Living is Easy.

When Victoria got back from UBC for the summer, every-one was happy to see her again. She and Jen and Wes slept in one room and talked and stood around the sink doing the dishes together. That was last month. Now they sleep in their separate rooms and fight like cats over who does the dishes. Meanwhile, I spend a lot of time at my desk trying to figure out if I will have some money left over at the end of the month.

Since Victoria started school, I've been very money conscious. I have a chequing account and a savings account. Just recently, I got a term account. Jennifer decided that school made her puke so she wasn't going to BCIT for Marketing/ Management. So I took the $5,000 in my savings account and pushed it into a term account. Term accounts pay more inter-est and are inaccessible for anywhere from ninety days to five years, so Wes and I won't be tempted to break into Jen's money (temporarily of course) and buy a computer or electric piano or three-wheel motorcycle with flotation tires (for the farm).

At the present time, saving money is not recommended by the government which has published statistics to prove that Canadians save far too much money. The government claims that if people just opened up and spent or invested more, then the economy would be stimulated and jobs created. I find this very suspicious. Formerly, the government was very much in support of saving. Also, as I understand it, the bank will invest the money I save anyway, so why shouldn't I let the bank take the chance? Maybe the bank is more careful than the government wants it to be. Maybe the bank has good reason to be careful.

As soon as Victoria got home, she went looking for a job. She is still looking. The trouble is, we are presently in a recession. This recession is hitting this town and young people in particular very hard. The trouble is that the economy here is based on natural rather than human resources. Human resources used to be muscles and brains but now they are mainly brains. Brains have put muscles out of business. Both natural and human resources are renewable, but only if you use brains. Unfortunately, the use of brains is not much appreciated here. The use of brains requires constant skepticism; everybody has got to ask and answer questions about everything. There has to be a lot of discussion and debate. You have to think. Unfortunately, thinking takes time away from really important things like watching TV, driving around in a truck and drinking. It is thought to be counterproductive and downbeat, best left to foreigners who are naturally argumentative, degenerate and devious. As a result of this attitude, there are no natural resources left and our reputation for brains has hit a new low.

This is particularly noticeable up north where we live. For example, Victoria was hoping to get a job in Tumbler Ridge where the new coal mines are. The coal mines were built in cooperation with the Japanese, who have their own coal but can't dig it up and burn it because that would reduce the size of Japan which is already too small. The Japanese are forced to use brains. They go around passing out computers and portable TV sets and talking about high technology. The politicians in resource-rich countries don't understand a word they say but they like the TV sets. In order to get more, they dig mines everywhere and then there is too much coal and the price goes down. Soon it takes a lot of coal to buy a TV set.

In B.C., the politicians put three-quarters of a billion

dollars of tax money into railways, roads and power grids into the coal mines. They built a new town full of pastel houses, with a pastel town hall dedicated to Tseuneti Nemoto who signed the deal for the Japanese. They got so excited signing, giving speeches, cutting ribbons, handing out contracts, laying tracks, building bridges and doing other enjoyable things, that they neglected to ask Tseuneti what he was willing to pay for the coal. Also, there was a geologist at the edge of the crowd telling everyone that they should wait a minute because the coal mine was in the wrong place. He was a local boy, however, so they told him to shut up or go away. He was trying to use brains.

If Victoria doesn't get a job, I will have to pay her fees again. The first installment is due in June. So far I have almost got enough. I have been cutting back on cafe meals. Also, I got a special deal on renting my ex-wife's house. She couldn't sell or even rent her house after she moved. Everybody in town is trying to sell. So she let me have it cheap. All I have to do is sublet the two basement rooms. In this way, she gets almost enough to pay the mortgage and any losses are tax-deductible.

While my kids are working or lying around the house, I take my summer vacation. Mostly, I stay on the farm, working on projects. This summer, I am adding a cement apron to the sundeck I built last summer. Once or twice a week I drive into town to see how the kids are doing. I do a few loads of wash, buy a pile of groceries, cook a meal or two, and straighten out any fights. Also, every summer I spend a week or two in Vancouver. This is where I am at present. I stay with my parents, buy books and visit friends.

I enjoy staying with my parents. They are old and have lived in Vancouver all their lives. My mother was born here and my father came when he was nine. My mother's family was in the drugstore business and worked their way from Ontario and across the prairies. Most of them are now old and in Victoria. My father came from Birmingham after the First World War when his father was demobilized. The old man cleaned out the chimneys at the gasworks near Georgia

Viaduct. They aren't there anymore. He died in middle-age and was buried in Mountain View cemetery.

Someday I hope to get my parents' memoirs on tape but so far I haven't had time. Also, I doubt my parents would tell me much. They think that their lives and Vancouver have vastly improved over the years. For them, the past is eminently forgettable. They live in their sunny house on Capitol Hill and go to Reno once or twice a year. They walk for five miles a day (doctor's orders). My mother takes the bus downtown, pays the bills and shops at Woodward's. My father cuts the lawn and washes the car. They remember all the birthdays and send presents and they put up all of their kids and their kids' kids whenever we come to town. Our rooms are all more or less the way they were twenty-five years ago; even our old university textbooks are still on the shelves. There are a couple more TV sets (colour) around, and a new washer and dryer and bathroom (with a shower) in the basement.

Once I settle at my parents' place, I eat a couple of my mother's meals and help my father wash the car. Then I am free to wander. One of my first stops is Bill's Bookstore in Gastown. Bill is a tall, skinny guy who wears horn-rimmed glasses and a Stetson. He is a great book collector. When I arrive he gives me a coffee and talks at me. This summer, he is very happy about the recent government funding cuts in the arts. He feels that this will greatly improve the cultural scene in this country. "They can't afford to keep all the vegetables alive anymore," he says. "They've been feeding them intravenously at great public expense for years. Now all these so-called writers are going to be unplugged. They'll be crawling around in the grass outside the universities and cultural institutions, legless, armless and certainly sexless. You and I will hunt them down and finish them off. BOOM! BOOM!"

The customers look up from their browsing. Bill's enthusiasm is making them nervous. Bill pays no attention. He deals mainly with serious collectors, and those who merely wander into his store have to take their chances.

I tell him I agree. I work my ass off to support my so-called writing and so can anyone else who doesn't make it in the marketplace. I ask him if he'll buy a dozen copies of a new book I have just written and published about Barry. I set it on the college computer, printed it onto mimeograph stencils and ran it on my old mimeograph. It's a rare interface, I tell Bill, of old and new technologies. He says that actually it's an interface of old and new garbage. He buys three copies.

While we are talking, Norm comes in. Norm is a poet who drives taxi. He is a good friend of Harvey's and asks me about him. I tell him that Harvey is looking better. His mother was sick for awhile and when she went into hospital Harvey went to the bar and got sick too. However, his mother is now at home convalescing and Harvey is working for Barry, painting and scraping the house. The sun and exercise are doing wonders.

"He wrote to me a couple of weeks ago," says Bill. "He says that the Canada Council is not relevant. 'The enemy destroys itself,' he says. He says that poetry is not a career, that the poet is an inmate in a concentration camp who moulds dried shit into cheese pieces. He believes you have to suffer to write. I can't accept that. Not much poetry is written in concentration camps."

"What is, though, is good," says Norm, sipping his coffee.

"It's not necessarily suffering," I say. "Remember what Blake said about 'the enjoyments of genius, which to the angels look like insanity.' Something like that. The cold never hurt Solzhenitsyn."

"It killed Babel and Mandelstam," says Bill.

"It's killing me too," says Norm.

I arrange to meet Norm and Bill later in the evening, and wander out onto Powell Street. The geraniums in the flower pots are bright red and green and the street is sunlit and happy. The office girls are out looking for lunch. I go to an underground arcade that has a barber shop, a health-food cafe, an international magazine shop, and a store selling handmade candies. I buy some chocolates for my mother-in-law and a New York design magazine for Jennifer. I get a coffee and sit at one of the sidewalk tables to read and watch the people.

Maybe my parents are right about the past. Gastown, for example, is a big improvement. Of course it is phoney and the cobblestone streets are (as Norm says) killers in the rain. But there are outdoor cafes with good coffee and there are international magazine stores. I remember riding my motorcycle through here in the early Sixties, on my way to and from the longshoremen's dispatch hall. The area was dark and smelled like burnt coffee. The buildings were all boarded up and used as warehouses. There was never anybody around.

While I am sitting at the sidewalk cafe thinking about the past, I see Connie. She is standing on the curb, dressed in a flowery white dress. She has ribbons in her hair. I wave and she sees me and comes over.

"I just had to get away," she says, sitting down and ordering a coffee. "There's a conference on Saturday at the Hotel Vancouver. The college wouldn't pay for it, but I convinced them to let me go if I paid my own way. I'm supposed to be doing professional development."

"Where are you staying?"

"I don't know yet. I just got here. I drove into Woodward's garage and left my car there. I stayed last night in Hope. It's so great to see leaves on the trees. And flowers! What are you doing here?"

"Visiting my parents."

"I always figured you were from the prairies or somewhere."

I tell Connie that I am looking for books and a graduation present for Jennifer. I tell her we should get together for a drink and I give her my parents' phone number. I tell her I don't know what to get for Jennifer. She says it should be something pretty, maybe a gold ring with her birthstone.

"I don't remember when she was born," I say.

"It's on your medical card," says Connie.

I like Connie. She leaves and I watch her walk away and think that it might be nice to fall in love with her. Alison has been gone for almost a year. I'm getting those urges again. Of course at my age you can't really call them urges. I get mainly happy letters from Alison. She is doing ok in pre-med, painting the new house in Calgary and looking after her kids. Connie seems like a reasonable person. She and Barry and I had a lot of fun during the staff strike in the fall. She is small and dark and full of energy.

After I buy a few books I go home. I take my parents to the White Spot for dinner. The White Spot is their favourite cafe. After that I go to Norm's place. He lives in a downtown hotel. When I get there I can't remember which door is his and there is nobody around, so I go back out to the street and wait for Bill or Brian to come along. Bill drives past in a VW bug, his Stetson crammed into the roof. He parks, goes into a corner store, comes out with a cigar in his mouth, crosses at the corner and walks towards me. We go up and he walks right into Norm's apartment without knocking.

Norm is pouring coffee in a sitting room overlooking the street. There is a big, younger guy sitting very stiffly in an armchair, holding a rolled-up pad of paper in his lap. We are introduced by Norm. Brian comes in and he and I shake hands. He is a writer who left the north years ago and did alright in Vancouver. He works for the city and publishes with all the small presses.

It turns out that Norm has a few people over every week to discuss writing. This is his contribution to Canadian literature. The meeting tonight is to discuss the big guy's new poem. This is why he looks so nervous. They have heard the poem before but it needs work. The big guy reads his latest version. It still needs work. Then Norm and Brian read. There are various suggestions for changes. I am surprised that they all have such a professional approach to their writing, but I wouldn't want to participate myself. As a matter of fact, it makes me nervous. I am happy when, after a couple of hours, we go down the street to a Greek cafe that serves beer.

The owner of this cafe follows all the poetry readings in town and loves to have Norm and his friends around. He has signed copies of their books in the shelves behind the bar. He is an example, Bill says, of legitimate patronage. I wonder out loud who's patronizing whom, but Bill says that, despite Harvey's opinion, money and art are not irreconcilable. We all get mildly drunk and the big guy reads his poem again. It sounds better this time and the owner is impressed.

I find myself thinking mainly about my parents. It occurs to me that they are not going to be around much longer. My father will probably go first. Over the past fifteen years he has had one major heart attack and three minor ones. He had the major one while riding his bike home after a day's work on the docks. He was cranking the bike up Capitol Hill. He put the bike down on the side of the road and walked to the nearest house. He told the people there that he wasn't feeling well. They let him lie down on their couch and phoned the ambulance. They went out and got his bike and later they visited him in the hospital. My parents are still friends with the people who helped my dad when he had his heart attack. My mother will probably last longer. She has a big heart in a small body, and a very placid disposition. In the thirties she worked for some of the biggest tycoons in the city, who are now dead and have buildings named after them, but ever since I've known her she's been at home making cookies and quilts and humming. She knows all of the old favourites from Rudy Vallee to Perry Como. My father says it's like living in an elevator.

Soon the owner's family is closing down the cafe. The owner shouts instructions at them from our table. The big guy signs the manuscript of his poem and gives it to the owner, who says he will frame it and hang it over the bar. He says his daughter, who is wiping tables, is a real poetry lover too.

Outside it is raining. Norm walks me to my truck and we say goodbye.

When I get home there is a note on my pillow from my dad. It says, "she called," and there is a phone number scribbled underneath.

The Windfall.

I never used to think much about money. I went to work and my wife looked after the house and kids and we slowly paid off any loans we got to buy our property, trucks, snowmobile, and roto-tiller. We always had a bill to pay but we never went hungry. When the kids got older and my wife and I split up, I became a saver. I holed up in cheap lodgings and babysat houses. I walked to work. I saved money for the kids' education.

In this way, I gradually became aware of money. Even though it was never in the bank for long there was always an account growing somewhere. I pored over my passbooks in the evening as I tucked into bed. This one represented another year of Nursing. This other one represented first-year Commerce. I dreamed of my kids with diplomas and degrees, and then with shiny Japanese cars and winter plane tickets to Hawaii. I even dreamed of unpaid leaves of absence, early retirement, a life dedicated to writing, cafes, friends, kids, and beautiful women.

Then I started to go out with Connie. She thinks about money even more than I do, mainly because she has more of it to think about. She and her husband both worked, and when they split they had two houses paid off. Connie sold hers and put the money into long-term investments. She has two daughters but they are not interested in university. Sometimes she buys them plane tickets or gives them the down payment for a car. They go from one job and boyfriend to another, living with various girlfriends in various flats and bothering their mother only when they raid her closet, borrow her car, get sick, or need counselling in long tête-à-têtes with dinner and wine in various Greek cafes.

Connie gets a substantial income from her money. Most of it stays in the bank and multiplies, but she uses some for a month of travel in the summer and a week in winter in the sun. She has been to China, Mexico, Ireland, Greece, Spain, South America, and Cuba. This strikes me as a very aristocratic way to live. Of course, if I had Connie's money, I would quit work entirely and go out to my farm to live in genteel poverty. Travel doesn't interest me. I figure that everywhere is much the same once you get beneath the surface. If I did travel, I would visit various cafes in various famous places where I would spend the afternoons drinking coffee, writing stories, and deciphering the newspaper. On the farm I would look out my window and watch the weather and write. I would cut wood and go to bed early. Maybe I would get bored and go nuts. What would I have to write about? I could get on my motorcycle and visit old friends.

Connie prefers to continue working. She says she needs her job for mental stimulation, though I don't see how you get any mental stimulation from teaching older kids how to teach younger kids. Also, by working she is able to add substantially to her money. Someday she will be able to spend all year travelling.

Connie and I discuss money on Saturday mornings on the farm. On Friday night, after work, we go to the bar for a couple of beer. Everybody talks about jobs and politics. Sometimes money comes up but usually it is in terms of the cost of new cars, motorcycles, videos, compact disc players, computers, and micro-wave ovens. Connie is pretty quiet during these discussions, limiting herself to remarks like "What do you need a motorcycle for?" or "I don't watch tv." She believes that all material possessions except for books, petit point, silverware, and good dishes are junk.

If the topic turns to travel, however, Connie is very interested, but she has to be careful because if she reveals all the places she has been or is going to, someone invariably says, "I don't see how you can afford it," and Connie doesn't like to talk about her money except to people like accountants, brokers, and lawyers who have a truly professional interest in it.

After a few beer we have dinner, and then we go to the farm in her car. I leave the truck with my kids so they can come out on Sunday if it's nice. We lug our stuff in and light the fire and drink some wine and jump into bed and make love if we can. When we wake up on Saturday we sit in bed with coffee and discuss money.

It was in the course of one of these discussions that I decided to sell the trees off the farm.

I wanted to be like Connie. For the first time in my life, I grasped the obvious fact that if you are always borrowing money, you are always behind. On the other hand, if you loan money, you are always ahead. It's simply a matter of getting into step. Compounded at present day rates, money doubles in value every seven to eight years. If you have $20,000 in the bank in your twenties, you'll be a millionaire by the time you die. There's a kind of mathematical purity to it.

Of course, even before I met Connie and became aware of interest rates, non-taxable investments, and the rest, I thought about selling the trees. Being visible from the road, they drew a steady trickle of loggers up our driveway, who just dropped in to see if we might be willing to sell. But we never were. We were attached to the trees. They had initially attracted us to the place. When we came to this area, we wanted to live in the bush. My wife went looking and, from a gravel road about fifteen miles from town, she saw a small pasture with a southern slope nestled against a block of tall pine. It was love at first sight, and it was all for sale. Once we moved onto the place, the kids built a tree fort in the pines, and they loved to sit out there and drink hot chocolate from a thermos. When the loggers showed up, the kids would stand around the table scowling at them, or would slip outside and draw Greenpeace symbols in the dust on their trucks. Once Jennifer wrote FUCK OFF on the truck of a very persistent and gabby logger, so we had to bawl her out for that.

After my wife and I split up, I got the farm and my wife moved out of town, and the kids and I rented her house, and the idea of selling the trees got more attractive. After all, I didn't see much of them any more. The kids hardly went to the farm. When they did, they stayed in the house and read their old comic books. If I sold the trees, I could pay off the rest of the mortgage. I could bank enough for a year at university. I could plant a money tree of my own.

By the time you reach your forties, you are very aware of money. You have been working for it and spending it for years, and in the not-too-distant future you will not be able to work for it any longer. This is of some concern in the sense that you are used to providing for all your basic needs by earning and spending money. Even if you have not given up on things like youth, wisdom, love, courage, hope, honour, and freedom, you have learned that you have to eat, sleep, etc. to have these things, and eating, sleeping, etc. cost money. Of course, at the same time, you know very well that this is a trap; money cannot really buy you any of these desirable things. As a matter of fact, any great concern for money can deflect your attention from the truly desirable and you will be fucked. If you are dedicated, the money will look after itself.

The trouble is that, generally, you are afraid. Maybe you are a slow learner. Maybe your body is weak or ugly. Maybe you are tired, sick, or old. Under these circumstances, money is, at least, a comfort. The more you have, the better your chances of avoiding disease, starvation, exposure, humiliation, and death. You will be able to feed your kids and provide them with bicycles, calculators, and piano lessons. You will be able to eat cafe meals and leave tips, buy wine, drive a nice car, and travel. You may not get happiness, love, and youth, but you will at least get satisfaction and respect, which are better than nothing.

So you hang onto your job. With luck and courage, you do some good, though it is more likely that you are stealing other people's money, fucking up their lives, boring them, and generally snuffing youth, wisdom, love, and courage. That is what working is all about. It is legalized theft, the weak ganging up on the strong, civilization preying on nature. If you have any strength, you hate it. Your satisfaction and respect begin to wear thin. You discover that your superiors are monsters, your colleagues dead, your life ugly, and your future dark. By the time you get to retirement, you are more likely to be steering a wheelchair or intravenous stand than a Winnebago or sailboat. Instead of writing novels, you are more likely to be writing obscenities on the wall with your own finger dipped in your own shit. Every morning it takes more coffee, hot water, shampoo, and deodorant to get you going. Every month you buy another piece of junk to bolster your self-respect. Every year your psychosomatic illnesses last longer. Your annual pension contribution remains the only obvious gain. Memories of love, courage, and youth depress you. You vote conservative. You distrust the young, the beautiful, the wise, the brave, and the happy. You read about the Third Reich, Treblinka, and the Warsaw Ghetto, and are struck by the common sense of murderers. You think you finally know what life is all about. You dream of anarchy, destruction, retribution, and the end of everything, especially your job. You pray for retirement, as early as possible, now, before the next batch of student reports comes in, before the alarm goes off.

I decided that the trees were my big chance. If I sold them, I could see myself in the future as hale, lonely, not a problem in the world, living on my paid-off farm, my kids educated. I would write, cut wood, ride my motorcycle, and fuck Connie when she returned bronzed from some exotic place in the sun.

Selling the trees was not easy. First, I had them estimated by a forestry consulting firm. They studied the aerial photos of the area and decided that there were 1000 cunits of merchantable timber on the place, for which I could get about $20,000. All I needed was a good lawyer to draw up a contract because, according to the foresters, all loggers are assholes.

After the estimates were in, Connie and I spent quite a few Saturday mornings discussing the trees. The trouble was, I could see them from the bedroom window. It's hard to talk about cutting down trees when they are in plain view.

"What would it look like when they finished?" Connie would ask.

"Like the surface of the moon," I'd say.

Connie would sip her coffee. "Right now," she would say, "money grows faster than trees." Then we would get into a discussion of the national debt, international loan defaults, free trade, and the problems of resource-producing areas.

The fact is, money is also safer than trees. Who cares about trees? The trees could've burned down someday, as they nearly did a couple of years ago when some guy was burning grass. The fire went across three quarters before it hit muskeg and stopped. Also, the lumber market was getting quirky. The Americans were thinking of putting up a tariff that would kill the industry. During the week we cut out newspaper articles on this and other economic matters, and on some weekend mornings, by the time we got bored with money and started kissing, the bed was covered with clippings and financial brochures.

Finally I advertised the trees for sale. I got three serious bidders. One was a logging contractor, the other a professional forester representing one of the local mills, and the other a horse-logger. The contractor took it. The mill came in lower and the horse-logger wanted to do it in partnership. Connie vetoed the horse-logger. It was too risky, even though the horse-logger would leave more trees standing and a lot of manure on the ground. "Always take cash up front," she said.

I sealed the deal at Bino's Pancake House. I had to resist the urge to ask the logger to be gentle. He smelled of pine resin and diesel fuel. It was near midnight when we shook hands, and then we sat and drank another coffee, and he told me about a doctor he'd found in Oregon who did a cancer treatment that had already saved the lives of two of his best friends. His wife was on it and doing fine. It was all in the diet.

The contract that he produced at Bino's didn't appeal to my lawyer. He was upset. "All it says is that he gets the trees and you get the money. What if he drives his skidder over your neighbour's place and does some damage? You need protection. There should also be clauses in here pertaining to Workmen's Compensation and standard Forest Service procedures."

"Yeah," I said. I was calculating how long the contract would be, at $50 a page. I was looking at the view. My lawyer was on the top floor of an office tower, in a corner office with floor to ceiling glass on two sides. The whole downtown was spread out below – Zellers, the Holiday Inn, about ten city blocks down to the railway yards, and then a blue strip of river and the cutbanks on the other side, with their fringe of dark-green spruce. It felt good to be part of all that action. At the same time, I felt a bit sick. It was getting near the end for my trees. I had a recurring image of a chainsaw biting into a tree trunk. I had a vague hope that maybe the logger would reject my lawyer's contract, rip it up and toss it on the floor, and then I'd ditch the whole idea or phone the horse-logger. "Make it tight," I told my lawyer. "Good idea," he said. "Most of those guys are real assholes."

There was no problem, as it turned out, with the contract. So far as the logger was concerned, any damn contract that suited me, suited him. He thought lawyers were a waste of time. Connie and I took it to his place one night and he signed it without even reading it. He lived on the main highway west of town, in a large ranch house that was beautiful except there was a row of rusty skidders and bulldozers on what should have been the front lawn. We met the wife and the grandson who were busy in the living room screwing together an aluminum Christmas tree. We toured the Winnebago, which was parked in the driveway. It had its own generator and a 100 gallon tank in case you couldn't get gas. You could drive over 1000 miles through hostile country if you had to. The office, as the logger called it, was on the other side of the carport and was filled by a huge pool table. Around the edge of the table were a colour tv set, a couple of recliner chairs, and a large crib board that also served as a coffee table. All the business records were in brown folders, stacked against the wall. The logger said he'd start before Christmas, as soon as he and the wife got back from Reno.

The logging was brutal. We were pretty quiet on those Saturday and Sunday mornings, half listening to the distant bellow of the skidder or the drawn-out wail of a chainsaw. To tell the truth, our sex life took a dive in those weeks. It was a mild winter, and the crew were highballing it to get out before the frost came out of the ground. We went out there a few times, but the sight of a skidder tearing around like a bucking horse, pushing over and grinding up the non-merchantable bush, made me sick. Once when it got quiet we went out to find the feller-buncher operator alone with his machine. He'd gotten behind on the falling because he got drunk on Friday night, and then he'd no sooner started on Saturday afternoon than he'd blown a tire. The rest of the crew had tidied up their end of it and gone for the weekend. He got real shit from the contractor for holding up the job. He said that another blowout would pretty well cost him everything he was likely to make on the job. Also, if spring came too early, he wouldn't be able to make his payments on the machine. We left him despondently tugging on one of the wheel nuts with a giant spanner, a six-pack of beer half finished on the seat of his truck, and the radio tuned to the local station.

It was the first time we'd been able to wander around without having to stay clear of the skidder. We found a small stand of birch trees that were all pushed over, their delicate white trunks pressed into the ground. I'd never seen these particular trees in among the others, and had always assumed that birch didn't grow on the place. The loader was parked beside a huge pile of logs, its giant claw arched high in the air. The skidder was parked behind the scrap pile. Beyond the landing was an impenetrable sea of broken stumps and branches. Connie was very quiet. We wandered around and finally started picking up all the sandwich wrappers, pop tins, and empty cigarette packages scattered around the landing.

Fortunately, it didn't take too long for the loggers to finish. In one month, fifty acres of pine were cleared off and nothing remained but the scrap piles and debris. Meanwhile, I had sent half of the logger's money to the mortgage company, and the farm was now mine. No more payments. I put $5000 into a 5-year mortgage certifcate. It wasn't much, but it was better than nothing. I felt like I was really on top of things. I had another $5000 to put with it, but hesitated. What if Victoria failed to get a good job in the summer? What if the college got hit by another strike in the fall? Also, I'd suggested to Wes that I'd spend a couple of thousand on a generator or a three-wheel motorcycle to make life on the farm more fun. We even went to the Honda shop to check things out, but I was scared. I didn't want to trade off the trees for any junk. We settled on the generator. Wes said he understood, but he did get a poster of a "Big Red" three-wheeler from the owner of the Honda shop, and put it up in his bedroom.

Connie wanted me to bank all the money. She was doubtful about the generator. She opposed the three-wheeler. "You could live for three months on what you'd pay for one of those," she said. "You could live for two weeks just off the interest."

This started me thinking. If Wes and I stayed on the farm and watched our expenses, we could last for a semester on the money we had left. I could avoid marking 600 tests and papers, at a half-hour each. I could give up trying to arouse the academic or literary interests of 150 bored teenagers. I could lower my income tax bracket and maybe write a novel. I could stay at home and stare out the window at my clearcut acres.

Report on the Nanaimo Labour School.

In August I got a free trip to Nanaimo. Nanaimo is one of my favourite towns. It has a seedy downtown area with lots of hotels and small shops where old hippies sell used books, brass beds, nickleodeons and hand-made guitars. The houses are all made of wood and are large and drafty. A doctor will live in one, a motorcycle gang in the next one and someone nearby will have a goat tethered to a tree. People who are into lawns, patios, Volvos and small dogs have abandoned Nanaimo for newer suburbs up and down the island. Tourists go in one end and out the other. They are into swimming, fishing and shopping centres, and a town with a pulp mill in the harbour and a coal mine in the past doesn't interest them. The town of Nanaimo has tried to capitalize on its historical past by putting a giant lump of coal in the centre of its downtown park. There is a plaque saying that this lump of coal was grubbed out of a tunnel that extended five miles out under the ocean bed, and there is a map of the tunnel. However, the lump of coal has not been a major attraction. Kids climb on it and get dirty. Nobody wants to think about people working, sweating, suffocating and being buried alive under tons of rock and water. Battles between unions and bosses are not as interesting as battles between armies. As compared to the bathtub races, which do attract crowds to downtown

Nanaimo for one drunken weekend each summer, Nanaimo's historical past is a dead-end.

However, Nanaimo has played a major role in my own life. A year after I got married, I went to Nanaimo to be interviewed for my first teaching job. I was at UBC at the time, a scant twenty-two years old, with a wife and one kid, and I was busy at a summer job as a research assistant. A kindly professor wanted me to concentrate on writing my Master's thesis instead of sweating it out as usual on the Vancouver waterfront, where all the polish laid on me in eight months of graduate school was erased in four months of running two-hundred-pound sacks of flour into the holds of Russian freighters. Every second word was "fuck" and I pronounced "po-em" as "pum." So I spent four hours a day lying in the sun on the clipped lawns of UBC, transferring the professor's marginalia from the 1848 edition of Coleridge's *Complete Works* into the 1964 edition. An exciting lady from the east, who happened to be the chairperson of an English department out there, came to visit the professor. It turned out that she had just terminated some poor soul for neglect of duty due to alcoholism, and she needed a replacement fast. She couldn't interview me on the spot, however, but invited me to breakfast with her on the following day at the Port O' Departure Hotel in Nanaimo. I went over there, ate bacon and eggs and got hired.

Years later, at that same Port O' Departure, with Brenda, who loved my stories, I (inadvertently) started a chain of events that terminated my marriage.

It occurs to me now, too, that my father was present on both of these historical occasions. On the first, he happened to be on his way up-island to Tahsis, where the International Longshoremen's and Warehouseman's Union was organizing. We crossed on the ferry together and he dropped me off at the Port O' Departure. The lady from the east invited him to join us for breakfast but he said that he never ate with a lady. At the time I thought this was rather droll and likely to affect my Career Opportunity but the lady seemed to find his comment charming. On the second occasion my father, by then retired, was on his way home from a fishing trip. He noticed an announcement that I was reading at the college and he dropped in to see me. He didn't come to hear my stories; he thought (and still thinks) they are shit. The next day, we took a long walk, had dinner, and went to see a play with Ian, an old friend of mine who had set up the reading. He had written the play for the B.C. Centennial, about Captain Cook and his men and how they spread syphilis to the indians. Ian's wife was the star, which seemed to explain to my father why the ravishing lady in the Marlene Dietrich costume would marry the dishevelled weirdo who liked my stories. Later on, as a matter of fact, after my wife kicked me out, my father got the idea that it was Ian's wife who had slept with me at the Port O' Departure. There was a hint of admiration in his anger. At any rate, during that time in Nanaimo with my father I was shaken and distracted by my experience with Brenda. My father recognized that something was wrong. When we said goodbye he reminded me that my main purpose in life was to look after my wife and kids, advised me not to drink when away from home and gave me a couple of shirts which didn't fit him any more because he was, he said, shrinking.

My father didn't turn up during my last trip to Nanaimo, and nothing portentous happened. In a way I wish something had, and in a way not, as usual. I was in Nanaimo on business. I went to a labour school, as a representative of our little faculty union, to study the recent changes to the labour code, hear about the situations at other colleges, and practise handling grievances. This is not the most interesting way to spend a weekend, but it isn't as bad as it might seem, and I was going to Vancouver anyway to pick up Connie who was flying in from Guatemala.

I arrived in Nanaimo early in the day. It felt great to be near salt water again. Sometimes I imagine myself buying a small hunk of sea-front on Sechelt or a Gulf Island somewhere but I remember from various boy scout camps that it rains like hell around there. Mainly, though, what stops me is that the whole area is a retirement colony for artists. They water roses, cut driftwood, build shacks with lots of windows, do interviews with the amiable idiots who host CBC talk shows, and produce endless amounts of shit until they are finally bored shitless with roses, driftwood, scenery, silence and the CBC and go back to the city to get a job. At that point their art, if any, improves significantly.

I drove straight from the ferry landing to the college to register for labour school. I was assigned a room in residence and told to come to a plenary session that evening, where we were going to exchange information on the labour scenes at our respective colleges. I dumped my stuff in the room and phoned Ian and arranged to meet him later in the bar. Then I walked downtown, had coffee and read all the newspapers. Then I found three bookstores and combed through them. I made it into the bar by three o'clock with a bag full of books to read. I was on my third beer and book when Donna walked in.

She didn't see me at first and I was too surprised to say anything. I hadn't seen her for two years. She wasn't much for writing letters; so far as I knew, she was still in Kamloops. She was obviously just finished her day in the finance company. She was dressed conservatively but sexily as required, and she had that haggard look on her face that comes from spending a morning writing up loans for people who will never be able to pay them back but will likely pay interest for years, and an afternoon making collection calls to people who swear and threaten various parts of her anatomy. When she finally saw me she ran right over and I got a warm hug and kiss that, I imagined, lingered significantly beyond the merely affectionate. She sat down and ordered her usual double vodka and soda and we settled in happily to fill one another in on the past two years and complain about our jobs.

At six o'clock Donna's boyfriend arrived and if he was not overly happy to see me, he didn't show it. He is getting used to our platonic relationship. He wants to get married but Donna is not ready yet though they have been living together longer than most people stay married. Then Ian arrived. He and

Donna got into a serious discussion about theatre. He was wondering if her company would finance a production but she didn't think so, not even if she were in it, unless of course Ian had a paid-off house or something to use as collateral. Ian admitted that he was in hock up to his eyeballs due to heavy support payments to two kids from two previous marriages and to his immediately-previous ex-wife who was in acting school. Donna suggested that, given the circumstances, his chances of getting a loan from anyone were as good as hers of becoming an actress. Ian thought her chances were not as bad as that. Finally, I proposed that we go and eat. The plenary session was already half over anyway. Hopefully, the other rep from the college had dutifully arrived to deliver the news.

Ian took us to a Mexican cafe. There we met some friends of his from the theatre and a couple from up north who knew Harvey and were already finished their enchiladas but came over to drink their coffee with us. The guy is a coroner. He told us that he was taking skin-diving lessons because a lot of his work on the island involves drownings. For example, they had recently fished up a Fisheries department diver who had apparently got caught in some weeds and, in the process of hacking himself out, had cut his airhose. His partner was busy on the other side of the pontoon and by the time he missed him, he was dead. But the RCMP said they figured the dead guy had been fucking his partner's wife and there had been a fight at his house the weekend before. "The cops didn't notice anything unusual and I doubt there was," said the coroner, "but I'd sure as hell like to see for myself."

We stayed at the cafe until midnight, and then went our separate ways. Both Ian and Donna and her boyfriend wanted me to stay over, but the last time I stayed at Ian's I got flea-bites. Ian always got to keep the dogs from his previous marriages. I doubted I'd sleep well at Donna's, for various reasons, not the least of which was the coroner's story and its possible application to my own case. Besides, I felt guilty about missing the plenary session. If I made it back to residence that night, I could be sure of getting to the morning sessions. I arranged to go to Donna's for dinner on the following day. Ian dropped me off at the college and gave me tickets to the next two plays in the local festival. He said that these were final performances and there would be parties afterwards at his place.

Next morning, I got up early and walked some paths in the college forest. Then I joined the labour school group for breakfast. There were two people from each college in the province and they were all standing around drinking coffee and babbling happily while they waited for breakfast. These are my colleagues and I feel great affection for them – for this group in particular because they work hard for the union. When we started in this business we were all very young and now we are growing old together, gracefully I think. We have all survived as teachers and that takes a good deal of imagination, and we have created a union that takes care of our professional concerns and sometimes even our salaries. Of course, while I always feel warm and secure when I am with my colleagues, I also feel that I am childish compared to them and don't quite deserve to be taken seriously, trusted with any great responsibility, or cared for as well as I am.

I was wondering what had happened at the plenary session. A lady from Dawson Creek hugged me and said she loved my story about the strike at my college but wasn't I bit hard on faculty? I started to worry about the effect of this story, which had gotten fairly wide circulation in a popular, slightly leftish journal. I started to wonder if they had discussed my story at the plenary session. Maybe I broke one of the ethical guidelines. Maybe they passed a motion that I would only find out about later when the minutes were circulated.

The fact is, I don't know my colleagues very well. Though I love them, I have trouble relating to some of their concerns. I've never been able to attend the regular TGIF beergartens sponsored by the union. To me, drinking beer in the college would be like fucking in a mortuary. I don't even drink coffee in the college. Also, my colleagues love to have cocktail parties, backyard barbecues, Christmas dinner-dances, New

Year parties, retirement parties (where the retirer is pre-
sented with condoms, Rhino Horn and Grecian Formula), in-
door beach parties in January and professional development
events to talk about New Approaches to Teaching. I have to
stay away from all these things. I am not interested if $200
kiddie seats are being stolen from the back seats of Volvos, if
there is too much chlorine in the pool at the fitness centre, if
there is a growing tendency for daycare workers to fuck children or if computers are useful in teaching composition.

On the other hand, I am always willing to vote more money
to the Faculty Fun Seekers. I attend all union meetings and I
have been a shop steward or member of the executive for as
long as I can remember. Once, in a crisis situation, I became
president and ran the union with, I think, some success. At
that time the incumbent president, who had originally beaten
me out in the election for the position by a vote of 90 to 6,
suddenly took a job in the new administration of our new
principal. Our principal is a very energetic (some say "charis-
matic" and others "psychotic") man who was making massive changes at the time as part of his new mandate. Because
of all the turmoil and paranoia, I and my executive were able
to rule by decree and levy unprecedented sums of money. We
used the money to hire a lawyer who was a friend of the
brassy young psychologist who was treasurer at the time. The
lawyer turned out to be very good at his work, and so did the
brassy young psychologist. We launched a number of actions
under the Labour Code and wrapped a few ropes around the
principal. We started the union on its present course of creative belligerence. Because of all this, I gained a lot of credit
which I have been frittering away ever since.

After breakfast, we all got down to a serious study of the
Labour Code. It was great to participate again in the idealism
and enthusiasm of my colleagues. My colleagues are very
professional. They possess and communicate the technique
and technology that keeps things going. They further believe
that this knowledge contributes to progress. They fight hard
to be allowed to communicate this knowledge in the best way.

You can mess with the salaries of my colleagues, but if you mess with class sizes, course content and departmental committees you are asking for war. Pensions are also sacred, but nobody's perfect.

As an example of the faculty attitude towards professional concerns, we believe that fifteen hours of lecturing per week, and class maximums of forty-five are not conducive to the exchange of information. When five office hours, twenty or more hours of preparation and marking, and another few hours of meetings are added to this, it is easy to see that faculty will be too irritable and irresponsive to teach. Of course they will do their best, but demoralization will slowly set in. They will start reading the textbook to their classes, using last-year's tests and writing rude comments on student papers. They will fall behind in research and publication and lose their love for poetry, math, science, etc. Eventually they will have mental breakdowns, drink excessively, or bumhole their students. My colleagues will use every trick in the book to prevent this from happening.

They are fairly good at these tricks. As professionals, they are patient, systematic and can produce copious amounts of standard English either verbal or written. However, they have one major weakness. They believe that everyone is educable. They would deliver briefs on the fifteen-hour lecture week to Adolf Hitler. If Adolf was confused or seeking information they would give him the same assistance they would give to Anne Frank. In other words, they have great faith in the redeeming power of reason and will do nothing to counteract it. They reasonably argue that the only way to foster reasonable behaviour is to be reasonable. To yell, swear, kick back, hate and plot complicated revenge is to play into the enemy's hands. What they sometimes fail to recognize is that their faith is also a vested interest that shades the fact that they do not have rationality entirely wrapped up. There are many fields of human behaviour like sex, friendship, love, money and even education where rational guidelines are often open to question or even despaired of. When my colleagues wander into these areas, they can be confused, overconfident and/or gullible.

This is not a complaint. If you can't believe in reason, what can you believe in? God? Mother Nature? Country? Love? Art? Karl Marx? George Washington? Don't make me laugh. Keep these in your dreams and they will do wonders and never get dirty, but when you are awake, think. Learn the best technique. Learn the proper behaviour. When I'm having my appendix out, do you think I want a politician or poet snapping on the rubber gloves? Am I worried about the state of the world? The nurse in the green mask is an angel. The doctor is God. Reason is my rock. However, I am weaker than my colleagues. I lack patience. I advocate the low blow. Hopefully I will grow out of this attitude in the not-too-distant future.

During that morning I learned what changes had been made by the slightly rightist fuckfaces who run the province and how these changes would likely affect grievance procedures. We were discussing these and other issues when I suddenly felt as if my bowels were being blown up by a bicycle pump. I barely made it to the washroom in time, and then I couldn't get out. It was the Mexican food. During the coffee break, the leader of my seminar group tracked me down. "Is that you?" he asked from the other side of the door. I told him what was wrong. He went back to the classroom and got my folder as well as all the information sheets that he was about to use in the next session. He shoved them under the door. "Read sections 93 and 125 of the code," he said, "and answer all the questions on the green sheet." This is an example of how understanding and accommodating my colleagues can be.

I spent the rest of the day in the washroom or at a nearby cafeteria table. I read through all the labour school material, the local student newspaper and one third of *Crime and Punishment.* By the time my bowels were settled, the labour school was shutting down for the day. I washed up and went off to Donna's for dinner. Of course, I couldn't eat or drink anything. I talked Donna and her boyfriend into coming to the play. After the play the cast had a party at Ian's. Ian took Donna and her boyfriend in hand and introduced them to everyone. I acted very responsibly and left early for my room. I couldn't drink anything anyway. I waved goodbye to Donna who was having a spirited conversation with one of the female leads. She smiled sadly at me and very gracefully blew me a kiss.

I slept well that night except I was awakened for a while at about 2 AM when some of my colleagues came in and crowded into the next room for a nightcap and some sandwiches. Fortunately for me, there were some visiting Japanese students on the floor above us and their group leader came down with the custodian and shut them up. I got up early and showered and was back in the college forest in time to walk the complete circuit and read about all the plants and fungi at each nature stop. When I got back down to the main campus, the cafeteria was still not open. I sat on a bench in the sunshine with the lady from Dawson Creek who told me gleefully that there would be some very sore heads at today's seminar.

Late that afternoon, the labour school closed except for some speeches from our executive that were scheduled for the next morning. My colleagues were meeting downtown for dinner but I was not up to eating. I phoned Ian but he wasn't in so I decided to go for a walk along the seawall. I'd walked that wall years ago with Brenda and I remembered how we paused for long periods to watch the boats coming and going. Then I remembered with even greater vividness how, the night before that, we'd walked away from the reading together discussing poetry, how we'd suddenly melted into one another's arms, how lost I was in her dark, naturally curly hair, how we'd made our way to the Port O' Departure, how slim she was, almost weightless, how her small breasts hardened when I kissed them, how her legs tightened around me and then (of course) how relatively ineffectual I seemed to be between recurring waves of panic, and finally how good it was to sleep warmly beside her and wake up now and then to see her peaceful face in the dark. I hoped she was still in love and loved, her breasts still hardening to someone's kiss. Then I thought about Connie and how long she'd been away, and how brown she'd be, her hair bleached by two months of tropic sun.

By the time I reached the end of the seawall my ass, scoured by yesterday's diarrhoea, was burning. I had to take a taxi back to Ian's. The play was great, and so was the party though I wished Donna were there to add a touch of real drama. When I got back to residence there was a note on the door telling me that, due to the number of delegates leaving that evening, the speeches scheduled for the next morning were cancelled. I was free to do whatever I wanted.

I lay down on the bed and started reading the Labour Code. I was disappointed.

Bonanza.

Reno is a dump. I heard rumours that on the outskirts there are beautiful residential areas set around giant shopping centres and parks, but I never saw any of these. So far as I know, in Reno there are no book and magazine stores, no international newspaper shops, no parks (except for a couple of green spots along the river), no art galleries, no museums, no movies and very few places to sit down. There are only hotels with casinos, and cafes. All the hotels are the same: highrise towers that fill entire city blocks, with casinos on the first two or three floors. The cafes are good but busy. You wouldn't want to sit there too long. The casinos are all that Reno is about. Coming in on the plane, you can see them glittering like cruise ships in the middle of the desert. They are open day and night. Messages like "Hourly Cash Draws," "Progressive Slots," "99-Cent Breakfast," "Free Valet Parking," and "World's Only Piano-Playing Pit Boss" leap across their giant marquees. No matter what hour of the day or night, the expectant crowds flow steadily in and out of their doors and up and down the streets between them.

Tourists come in by the thousands on tour buses or charter flights. Most are from California or Canada. Most are elderly. They gamble steadily but modestly on the quarter or nickel slots, pumping the handles or picking at the video poker buttons. Every once in awhile, the bells ring and the lights flash and the pit bosses run over with microphones and buckets and a dazed but lucky pensioner is led off to the cashier's booth to collect the jackpot. The other players look up wearily from their machines and hope that soon it will be them.

I took my parents and my aunt Irene to Reno. It's their favourite vacation spot. I bought four tickets – for $250 you can fly to Reno and back, staying for four days in a nice motel. When you consider that the motel alone would normally cost you $250, this is a good deal. Furthermore, you get enough coupons to eat for nothing. Drinks are free while you are playing the slots. Of course, it's not the sort of thing I would do by myself, but I love spending time with my parents and aunt. They will not be around forever. They looked after me until I was twenty – my aunt replacing my dad for a few years during the war. They are very cynical – especially my father who made himself unpopular on the plane trip by claiming that in Reno you could sometimes feel the ground shaking from underground nuclear tests, and that he had seen dealers with three arms and even a three-legged stripper. But despite their acid commentary, they dream of the big jackpot. They want to give it all to me and their other kids and their grandkids. They hope to do even more – everything – for all of us.

My mother is the only one with any luck. Of course I don't mean luck in the broadest sense. All of us are lucky in this sense, so far, except perhaps my aunt who still pines after Uncle Joe who died thirty years ago of cancer, leaving only a safari jacket and complete sets of Pogo digests and Eric Nicol books, all of which have been passed on to me. I mean luck in the sense of getting money. In our society, more (they say) than in any other, all great human attributes can be measured in terms of money. While we all know that money can't really measure any of these attributes, we also know that time is short and qualitative measurements highly personal. Quantity, on the other hand, is easily counted. Since money is numerical and the official medium of exchange, it is a natural measure. What it lacks in subtlety it makes up for in power. Lucky people may be famous, smart, beautiful, loved and free, but if they are poor they are not lucky. Unless you have money, your luck, wisdom, talent, knowledge, looks and personal appeal are definitely open to question.

According to what little I know of probability (the only university math course that I succeeded in passing), there is no reason why my mother should so consistently be the lucky one. The only tangible difference between my mother and my father, say, who will push his day's limit of $50 into the dollar slots until it is all gone (which usually takes about three minutes), is that my mother has a system. She plays machine poker only. If the machine doesn't "let her in," as she puts it (that is, give her some winnings), after three hands, she goes to another machine. She plays the machine as long as she wins enough to continue without putting in any more money. If she wins, she stops at $200, cashes in and goes to another machine. She never plays dollar machines, but goes for longevity. "You can only be lucky if you are still playing," she says. Also, her system gives her the illusion of control; she is better able to avoid, or postpone, the despair of losing.

I was afraid I would prove to be a compulsive gambler. I would go crazy, put down my life savings, bid the farm and sell my kids into slavery. The stakes seemed high. If I won big I could take more time off, buy a three-wheeler, quit my job, spoil my kids even more than I do now, make generous gifts to friends and relatives, travel with Connie, freely pursue my hobbies and, in general, increase my quota of freedom, luck, love, fame and happiness. On the other hand, if I didn't win, it was more of the same.

Fortunately for me, I was turned off by gambling. First, it bored me. Even when I was winning, I wanted to get it over with so I could read a book, eat breakfast or go for a walk. Second, I knew I was being taken. This fact was, of course, a major topic of conversation among the gamblers, but the bottom line was that, if the casinos made money (enough, they said, to pay for all the roads, schools and hospitals in Nevada), then the gamblers lost it. Altogether, I plugged $400 into the machines, and won back $330. By the time I left Reno, I considered myself lucky.

After the first morning in the casinos, I needed a change. The strain of keeping track of my money got to me. The noise and flashing lights gave me a splitting headache. So I started to walk all over Reno.

Reno reminded me of my town except we have pulp mills instead of casinos. Most of the gambling in my town is done in real estate, since the mills are owned and controlled from elsewhere. With real estate, all you have to do is bet on the upturns and downturns of the economy. A few win very big but most lose, though usually modestly. Nobody knows what the corporations that run the mills will do next. If they cut production, the town collapses. If they increase it, it booms. Most of my colleagues didn't guess right. They are paying off an extra mortgage or two. They hung on to these investment properties too long and now the values are declining rapidly, though of course the payments stay the same. But there is always hope for the future.

In my walks around Reno I found one movie theatre. I found a playhouse but nothing was on the bill except acting lessons for kids. I found a massive outfitting store for cowboys, where Lorne Greene and the boys of the Ponderosa bought their boots, etc. I was surprised to discover, here and in other stores, that Lorne has the status of a local hero. This made me, as a Canadian, feel ambiguous. Though Lorne is a fellow Canadian, I have to admit that he knows as much about acting as he does about cows.

I noticed a number of things that you don't see in Canada, like "Honest Ed's Bail Bonds" across from the Police Station. The hospital was advertising a special on deliveries and the chapel a divorce-marriage package. I started to wonder what would happen if I got sick or broke the law. Would they take my medical card? Would I get a deal on a used kidney? Would Ed give me bail? On the other hand, I saw some cottonwood trees, some Canada geese buzzing in formation up and down the river, and a long line-up of ragged men at the mission. These things made me feel more at home.

Besides walking, I spent a lot of time getting my aunt and parents to and from the various casinos. I would meet them at a certain time and chaperone them to another place. They can't make it across a two-laned street before the light changes, and my dad and aunt have to stop a lot and pop nitroglycerine. They like to visit all the casinos in order to pick up the free tokens and meal and drink tickets that are given out to people on charters. This involves numerous shuttle-bus trips to the outskirts of Reno where the desert starts. We spent the mornings on these trips, and I usually put my parents on the bus around noon and walked back into town myself. Also, my aunt and parents always take an afternoon nap, so I chaperoned them to and from our motel in the afternoon. Finally, meals took up a lot of our time. My parents and aunt are always searching for a decent pot of tea, a thing unheard of in the U.S. where waiters and waitresses merely run the hot water tap for a second and fill the pot. Fresh hot water has to be demanded and then there is a lot of mashing of teabags and getting refills. Also, misunderstandings often occur because American waiters and waitresses are waiting for a "yes" or "no" response to their questions whereas we Canadians say "maybe" (meaning "yes if you coax me") and "I don't know" (meaning "no unless you can convince me otherwise"). Rather than taking this as a cue to engage in friendly conversation, American waiters and waitresses take it as a cue to leave and come back later for a straight answer.

On the third day, having criss-crossed Reno two or three times, I decided to go off on my own and see the surrounding area. I took a day-long bus tour to Virginia City, Carson City and Lake Tahoe. The bus was packed with ladies attending a convention of elevator salespersons at the Sands Hotel and a number of gamblers like myself who were either tired or broke but still had some time to put in before they could go home. The ladies wore their name tags and were lively and the

- 112 -

gamblers were tired and cynical. The driver was a talkative fellow who strayed from his prepared script to indulge in numerous personal anecdotes and jokes. He was obviously a veteran and spaced his script and quips for maximum effect. He created a certain esprit de corps right off by announcing that we would breakfast in one hour at Virginia City. He said he couldn't vouch for the quality of the breakfast but that it was entirely free, no obligation. He said his company understood that the only people who signed up for these tours were people who had nothing left in their pockets but their ticket home. He implied that he was a bus driver for much the same reason. He proved his point by asking any winners to put up their hands. No response. Then he asked for the losers. Everyone responded. Soon people were cheering as the losses were announced, right up to a man who had cleared $1000 at "21" and then lost it and another $500. "I couldn't get him away from the table," the man's wife said. "He was looking down the dealer's dress." "It was worth every cent," said the man proudly.

Virginia City is the historical metropolis of Nevada. In the 1850s they discovered veins of pure silver in the ground that were as thick as telephone poles. They mined it out, leaving only mountains of tailings, a ghost town about four blocks square, and a cemetery that rolls out over the surrounding hills as far as the eye can see. During its heyday, Virginia City was the biggest town west of somewhere. Mark Twain worked on the local newspaper. Randolf Hearst's father started the family fortune. Wyatt Earp dealt cards. The Studebaker brothers built their first wheelbarrow. Levi invented jeans. Michaelson, who got the first U.S. Nobel Prize in physics for discovering the speed of light, was educated at the Fourth Ward School, the first American school built with movable walls. The place, in short, was a hive of creativity. The U.S. government built a mint there, and the bus driver informed us that the Comstock lode paid the bill for the Civil War. I doubted this, but it just shows how much money was made there.

The driver took great delight in telling us passengers about the historical details. His take on it was humorous. He pointed out that Mark Twain was kicked out of town for challenging someone to a duel. He and his adversary both left in the middle of the night, instead of doing the honourable thing of meeting in the sagebrush at the outskirts of town and blowing one another away. So it is unlikely that they really wanted to add to the acres of tombstones around town. He pointed out that the prostitutes were the best and most interesting of the citizens of Virginia City, which (he said) may be why prostitution has always been legal in Nevada. They were the social workers and nurses. He also pointed out that the town's population was now about 300, and that the only silver presently being mined in the area was the silver that he bussed in every day.

This was a timely warning, because as soon as we arrived the bus was invaded by the host casino owner who was to give us the free breakfast. He gave a long, excited speech about how it was Canada Day in Virginia City, Canadian money was being taken at par, and $100,000 had been won at his place since the first bus rolled in at 9 AM. Sure enough, there was a maple-leaf flag and a picture of the Queen in the casino dining room. The elevator ladies, who obviously had not been in Nevada for very long, got quite excited. However, the breakfast was spoiled because they had run out of sausages and coffee. Also, the pensioners who had been there before spread the word that you got par only on tokens which had to be used in that particular casino. The pensioners looked knowingly at one another, ate their eggs, and got out of the casino and into the cafes up and down the boardwalk. After toying with the slot machines for a few minutes, the elevator ladies followed their example. They all wandered up and down the wooden sidewalks, comparing notes on where the best coffee and souvenirs in town were.

I walked through the graveyard and finally ended up in a small park beside the burlesque theatre. There was a tiny bandstand, that would hold maybe a tuba player, and one bench. The bus driver was sitting on the bench, reading the paper, eating a bag lunch and drinking coffee out of a thermos. I wanted to ask how the park got there but thought it would be unfair to bother him during his break. It was strange to see him so silent and unprofessional, munching on a sandwich. I quietly opened my book and we spent an hour together on the bench in the warm sun.

After Virginia City we came down out of the mountains. The country was empty but the remains of fairly recent settlements were everywhere, a litter of mineshafts, quarries, boarded-up garages, cafes and hotels and burnt-out cars and trucks, their bodies shot full of bullet holes. The bus driver was quiet through all of this. I assumed that nothing of any historical significance had ever happened in this area. At one point, a very slovenly-looking road crew kept us waiting for almost an hour while they did some imperceptible thing to the road. They kept waving at the elevator ladies who didn't wave back.

I fell asleep and when I woke we were at the outskirts of Carson City, the capital of Nevada. The bus had stopped suddenly in a large parking lot. A sign said "Carson Ranch For Men Only." The driver told us that this was a brothel. It was one of many, each with its own airstrip, bus station etc. He told us that he had never driven any buses there himself, but assumed that he probably would in future as the brothel business was, as he put it, growing in leaps and bounds. He wondered if there would be any fringe benefits. There were girls just inside the door, waving at the bus. There was a VISA sign on the door. The man who had lost $500 started shouting "Open the door! Let me off!" but his wife shut him up. The driver said there were also ranches for ladies only but he refused a request to show us one.

Other than the ranches, Carson City (named after Kit Carson, who camped there for awhile) has only the state legislature and government buildings, a couple of giant prisons and the boarding house where John Wayne filmed *The Shootist*.

The last stop was Lake Tahoe, on the California border,

the biggest alpine lake in the world. Alpine lakes, the driver informed us, are defined as any lake situated over 8000 feet. There is enough water in Tahoe to supply all the domestic water needs of the U.S. for five years. It would take 200 years to refill it from its natural sources. Lake Tahoe is at the centre of a Ponderosa Pine forest. In the old days, there was a lot of logging in the area. Logs were skidded up to the top of the ridge, shot on a flume down to Carson City, floated across the small lake there and then skidded up to Virginia City.

I asked a lot of questions about the flora and fauna in the area, and the bus driver knew a lot about this and about the indians who had originally lived there. He pointed out a cliff along the lake which seemed to contain hundreds of indian faces. This cliff had been a sacred place and the indians had used the lake at that spot to bury their dead. The lake water was so cold that it preserved corpses for a long time. The faces on the cliff were said to be the faces of the indians buried in the lake. Every time they dropped one in, a new face would be discovered on the cliff. The indians came here to worship and mourn their dead. The bus driver advised everyone that, if they put their hands against the windows as the bus went through the cliff, they might receive messages and visions from the dead indians. Everybody put their hands on the glass. When the bus came out of the tunnel, the driver asked us if we felt the pain. This joke came off very well.

At present, Lake Tahoe is a popular resort area sporting two stern-wheelers and (on the Nevada side) two huge casinos. We stopped for lunch there. We each got a voucher worth $5 and five quarters (which I used for dessert) for the slots. After lunch I explored the town but was disappointed to find that the lake was fenced off. The beach was private property. However, on the way back to Reno the bus stopped at a public boat launch near the end of the lake and I dipped my hand in. It was cold. Nearby was the meadow where they filmed the opening credits of *Bonanza*. It was here that Lorne and the boys rode hard up to the camera while the music boomed. On the highway there was a foodstand selling

"Hossburgers," but I remembered that Hoss died shortly after the series ended and I decided to stick to the coffee. I picked up a fresh Ponderosa pine cone, though, that was almost the size of a football. I figured Wes would like it.

Coming back into Reno, half the bus was asleep, but the driver kept up his monologue. We learned that Reno was a random choice of a name, suitable to a town that specializes in random choices. The names of a bunch of Civil War heroes were thrown in a hat and that of Col. Jessie Reno was drawn. He never saw the place. We were shown steam pouring from the ground and heard that the state was about to "curtail" the steam to make electricity. I fell asleep again and woke up only when the bus stopped in front of the hotel. My aunt and parents were there waiting for me. They looked tired but had some good coupons for dinner, and my mother had cleared $200.

None of us gambled that evening. We went back to the motel and watched TV together in my mom and dad's room, and then we went to bed early. We had to be out of our rooms by 11 AM the next day, but our plane didn't leave until 11 PM, so we would have to spend many hours wandering around without having a nap.

I was very restless that night, my mind full of images of the bus tour. I gave up trying to sleep. The highway crew bothered me. They seemed so far away from the hustle and bustle. I wondered if they all lived out there in the hills among the ruins. They looked ragged and run down. Maybe they were all compulsive gamblers. I wondered about the faces on the sacred cliff and how they felt about the four-lane highway that carried all the commerce of Nevada through their entrails. I thought of Lorne Greene. There had been many pictures of him around Lake Tahoe. In the foyer of the casino where I ate lunch, he was pictured in a full-size cardboard cutout, wearing a magnificent cowboy outfit. At least he was making a living. Too bad there were no indians left for him to fight. I never saw any indians in Nevada. Yet the faces on the cliff seemed to be waiting for something. Maybe the indians were still there somewhere, back in the hills. Someday, when the traffic, gambling and underground tests end and things get quiet, maybe they'll come out from behind the tombstones, bushes and dilapidated walls and the faces of the road crew and visit the sacred cliff. Maybe they'll get tired of waiting and they'll come out soon, joined by tired pensioners, broke gamblers, men from the mission line-up and three-legged strippers, all those who won nothing or lost everything. Maybe Lorne will lead them. Then again, maybe he and his men will hold out bravely in the casinos, defending their pensions and civilization as we know it.

I wonder which side my parents would take? As for myself, knowing what I know, and given the chance, I'd probably join the indians. Not that I hope for any better, but it would be a change.

The next day, we took it very slow and made it to the airport at last. My mother took in another $200, my dad lost his $50, and my aunt and I broke even. We got rid of the last of our American change in the airport, trying to win a three-wheeler for Wes. It was suspended above a cluster of flashing slot machines. I noticed that it hadn't been dusted in a long time. "What do I do if we win?" I asked my Dad. "Drive it to Canada?"

"You're a teacher," he said, "you got time."

We didn't win the three-wheeler, and at Canada Customs in the Vancouver Airport they politely took my pine cone away. The officer explained to me that Ponderosa cones can carry deadly plant diseases that could decimate the forests of B.C. He dropped the cone in a plastic-lined garbage bag beside his desk.

I've Got To Do
Something About My Life.

My father had a minor heart attack on Sunday. This was his fourth minor after one major that he had fifteen years ago. Under the "Compassionate Leave" section of the collective agreement, which allows me five paid days per year in the event of death or illness in the immediate family, I rushed down to be with him and my mother.

The funny thing was, Barry had just been through a similar scenario. His mother had gone in for a heart operation that got complicated due to emphysema due to smoking. Barry went to Calgary to see her. The operation wasn't a success so he had to hang around waiting to see if she would live or die. While he was waiting she had a stroke. It was touch and go. He went over the five day allotment so we arranged to cover classes for him. He sat in the hospital with his dad, waiting for his mother to come and go in and out of consciousness. He hit the jazz bar at night and saw some old friends but his heart wasn't in it. Finally he had to come home with nothing settled, leaving his dad alone in the corridor staring at the wall.

I was thinking about this during the flight to Vancouver. I was particularly concerned about my mother, who sounded upset and distracted over the phone even though it is a tradition in the family to keep feelings and problems hidden. I started to wonder whether I would ever have to live in

Vancouver, which is a real shitpile, and look after her in the event of my father's death. If I did, how would I earn a living? This led me to wonder whether I will ever be a famous writer and (if not) whether I will ever have enough money to retire. By the time the plane landed, I was calculating how much the trip was going to cost and what I would do to cover it until next payday and the one after.

Victoria picked me up at the airport. It was worth the whole trip to see her, even if my dad was in trouble. Anyway, she immediately calmed my fears on that point, "I think he's coming out of it," she said. "I was there yesterday watching him and he woke up and smiled and said, 'No use hanging around, Vic. It all goes to Grandma.'"

I laughed. My dad always did like to foster the comic side. That's what I love about him and all the people I love. They're tired, bored, aging, scared and as happy as can be.

Of course my own concerns about money, fame and the unfolded future vaporized while I was visiting my mom and dad. In the face of sickness and death, they all seemed funny. After all, what sort of guarantees am I looking for? How much money is likely to be enough? Obviously, you can always use more. As for my retirement plans, they will probably get pulled apart by forces beyond my control. I hope they do. What generation ever got what it thought it deserved out of life? What generation ever deserved more than what it got? What are the chances that my generation will get to live out its mainly silly dreams? The highways are already cluttered with motor homes, tour buses and geriatric motorcycle gangs. Airlines are booked solid with tours to Reno, Florida, Disneyland and England. Traffic is backed up by people with white hair who can't make it across the street before the light changes. Pension funds are strained to the limit. Obviously, the younger generation would have to be pretty stupid or altruistic to put up with much more of this. Anyway, the actual chances of avoiding mental, physical and economic illness long enough so that everything is suitably arranged and the delicate flame of youth carried safely into old age, so that life isn't just the afternoon news, the follow-up and the soaps, is very slim. In fact, the whole idea could be a contradiction. Unlike love, sex, fame and wealth, retirement is not a goal likely to inspire a great deal of regenerative mental and physical activity through adult life. In short, the harder you try for it, the less likely it is that you will really get it.

I thought about this while sitting outside the ward waiting for visiting hours or for my dad to wake up, and while driving with Victoria to and from the hospital past rows of colourful houses and lines of shiny cars in the Vancouver rain. I think about these questions a lot. Barry and I often adjourn to the Sears cafe between classes to go over it and sometimes we meet Harvey and others at the bar, though as time goes on we seem to be drinking less and sleeping more. We all agree that we are facing a major question, perhaps the root existentialist dilemma. "All I know," says Barry as he digs into some bacon and eggs or lifts a beer, "is that I've got to do something about my life."

On the one hand, Barry and I bought the package: job, marriage, kids, pension. We are the rock upon which civilization is built. Since civilization is of dubious value, we suffer the usual angst. It is not at all clear that keeping teenagers out of the shopping malls and off the streets during business hours is a positive contribution. While we pay taxes so that people who have heart attacks can go to the hospital, we also contribute to nuclear arms, acid rain and corporate profits. If civilization is the means by which the crazy organize the weak to exploit the strong, are we men or mice? Of course we want to be writers but who doesn't? We have learned not to talk or think about that.

On the other hand, Harvey, and a significant number (Barry and I have noticed) of his contemporaries, have definitely rejected the package. They live on the edge. They watch people like me and Barry go through more money in a year than they do in five, and enjoy the benefits of computers, motorcycles, videos, kids and the latest in leather jackets and walking shoes. They live in basement suites and their parents' rec rooms and wear clothes from the Sally Ann. One of Harvey's old school buddies, Wally (the Wanderer), has gone so far as to detach himself almost totally from here to live for six to eight months each year in Latin America. He works in the bush in winter and then he's gone. He says things are cheap there. He says it's the future and he was always the curious one. He can't wait to see it.

On his last trip he saw too much of it. Crossing the border from Nicaragua into El Salvador, he had the shit kicked out of him by a bunch of jackbooted, teenage border guards. He came close to having some large holes bored in him but got off with a broken nose and a few cracked ribs. It was all over the T-shirt that he picked up in Managua and was thoughtlessly wearing as he crossed the border. It had a picture of a peasant family standing together in a field watching the sun set or maybe rise. "Turns out that in Salvador they hate peasants," said Wally. "Maybe if their asses were up instead of their heads it would've been ok."

Harvey and Wally are always willing to listen to Barry and me whine about our jobs. They take a clinical interest in aging liberals. Harvey says that until he met us he couldn't figure out what was wrong with the world. Also, they understand from their own (relatively limited) work experience that only those people who are after a number of vicarious gratifications could actually enjoy their jobs. At some point, though, if we go on too long, they get bored and ask why don't we just quit. Of course, when they ask that, they then have to listen to a litany of reasons that don't add up. Obviously, our kids can live without cars, motorcycles, rear-entry ski boots, stereos, videos and even university educations. These things are as likely to fuck them up as make them happy. Obviously, our pensions will not be secure no matter how big they are.

Harvey and Wally really believe that you can do whatever you want. There's no one to be responsible to, least of all the so-called system which couldn't get much worse or better. "We've just been very lucky," Wally says. "It's got nothing to do with democracy, capitalism, brains, work ethic, religion, etc. They've got all that down there. They've got tons of it. It's just that we got to gut out, using the latest equipment, the last livable part of the world. What'll we have left after we've finally cut down, dug up, poisoned, polluted and sold off everything? Freedom of speech? Unions? Parliamentary democracy? Don't make me laugh. We'll have one big mind-fucking debt. The more you make, the more you spend, as we all well know. Instead of fighting over the profits, we'll be fighting over the debt. We'll be killing one another to pay it off."

"I can see why they shoot guys like you down there," says Barry.

"Guys like me tend to head for the hills," says Wally. "When things get really bad we join up with the crazies in the jungle who are learning how to shoot Chinese guns. It's guys like you that they usually shoot. One thing a fascist or commie hates even more than peasants is teachers and artists."

"What did we ever do to them?" sighs Barry.

"What did you ever do *for* them? You're supposed to be serious. You're supposed to believe in the immediate crisis and shoulder the fucking load. You're not supposed to ask questions. You're not supposed to moon around thinking about it. Right now it's the debt. The only thing you're supposed to know is that the debt is bad. It's too big up here, but down there they couldn't pay it off even if the whole population of the U.S. was hooked on cocaine. They couldn't pay it back even if every man and woman in Latin America blew every woman and man in the rest of the world at ten bucks (American) a job. In a hundred years their combined debt will be more than the accumulated assets of the world. In two hundred years, it will surpass the total mineral value of the solar system converted into TV sets, videos and sports cars."

I'm usually silent through this kind of talk. I still have a certain attachment to institutions. I'm still on the inside looking out. Barry is too but he pays more psychologically and dreams of the apocalypse. At work, he gets heavy migraines and bumps into walls and doors. He sweats until his shirt is stuck to his back. He can't look at a computer monitor without puking. He drinks too much coffee and gets faint before class. He lies awake at night thinking about lectures, assignments and the Phys. Ed. majors in the back row who turn their Walkman radios up too high and toss paper balls back and forth.

I, on the other hand, work on union committees and go to all the meetings. I sit there doodling lines, looking out the window and sipping free coffee. I sit in the can for hours staring at the door. I slip into the gym between basketball games and have a shower. I find the walls and central heating comforting. Furthermore, I take great comfort in shopping centres, the police, my dentist, my kids' teachers, and the doctors, nurses and equipment that are looking after my dad. I'm actually not as good at my job as Barry, who can get people really excited about poetry. But I get by. I kick a few students out of class during the first weeks of semester. I get them laughing. I administer regular multiple-choice tests. I give them all "B"s. I hope that, if I can just stick it out, I will be safe, one of the rare recipients of the benefits, sitting in the shade sipping coffee while others are whipped out into the sun to pick it. Poor devils, but someone's got to do it. Granted that no amount of money, fame, sex, love, security, etc. will ever satisfy any one person, and that few will ever figure this out and settle for less. Granted that the only right we really have, because it is the only one we all unfailingly take for ourselves, is the right to cheat, steal, murder and (mainly) hoist our assholes whenever and wherever told to do so in order to get what we think we want. Granted, in short, that we are what we are.

I have to admit, though, that I'm not as safe as I once was or thought I was. As a matter of fact, few of us at the college are very happy. We got a good salary but we're still broke. We got educational leave and professional development time but no one can think of anything much to do with it. We got seniority but we hate our work. We got early retirement but we can't afford to go. When we negotiated these benefits, we didn't really count on getting old and tired. We suspect now that these are merely the intimations of mortality; the real shit is still to come. Those of us who have tried to escape the common fate have failed dismally. Due to the housing market collapse, my colleagues who bought more expensive houses in the hope of selling out more profitably in the future, are paying increasing amounts of money for decreasing value. Those who invested in extra houses and rented them to immigrants are not getting enough rent to do repairs and pay off the mortgages. Those who went into the stock market held on until their hands were empty. Ownerships in cafes, bookstores and bakeries led to lawsuits, heartaches and loss. Marriages split up and spouses ran off with properties, incomes and pension funds and were usually replaced by other spouses who also ran off or who brought or resulted in new families, so that colleagues who had just helped beloved sons or daughters emerge from universities with degrees and futures are also dropping perhaps equally beloved but maybe not nearly so interesting infants off at the daycare centres every morning.

I've learned a lot about my colleagues since last year when Barry went on leave. Before that we sat in the same office, wore one another's sports coats and entertained one another. We were self-sufficient. Rumour went around that we were a couple of closet homos. Then Barry got leave and Robin took his desk and then when Barry came back I gave him my desk and moved in with Kurt. Barry couldn't go in with Kurt because Kurt eats some kind of powerful sausage every day for lunch, has long phone conversations with his wife about the amount of butter she puts on his sandwiches, regularly checks and announces his blood pressure, likes to talk about existentialism, tragedy, conservatism and suicide and keeps shorts and running shoes in the office so he can work out in the gym every day. Any one of these habits, to Barry, is like masturbating in public. Neither Robin nor Kurt have ever been on leave whereas Barry and I have each been twice. They can't afford it.

Robin is a political scientist with a fine sense of irony and a spirit of élan that never fails him. He is very comfortable with students and never refers to them as "outcomes" or "the little buggers." However, he seems to have given up on political science. He has all the great books beside his desk – Machiavelli, Hobbes, Mill, Marx, etc. – and can even be seen in a quiet time, when not asleep, browsing through them. But he never talks or writes about these books or any contemporary theories. Actually, he doesn't even teach political science anymore. He teaches English to foreign students.

Five years ago, Robin was laid off and all of his courses were cancelled. He received a healthy severance package (half a year's salary) and took a course on selling insurance policies that provide a university education for your kids. He stopped being a teacher and became an Education Consultant. If you died the moment after you signed up, Robin's policies guaranteed your kids a bright future. Who could refuse a deal like that? Many did. For one year, Robin wandered the streets and office towers of Vancouver and lived with his parents in his old room. Once in awhile he would turn up back in town to visit his (third) wife, do some work on the house they had just built and stop at the union office to see how the grievance concerning his layoff was coming along. Meanwhile, Robin's various payments to his previous wives lapsed and the bank tacked the mortgage payments that Robin couldn't make onto the principal amount until his equity in the house shrank to nothing and then minus nothing.

There was never a word of complaint from Robin. Perhaps political science had taught him something after all. Also, when he was in Vancouver he got to visit the sailboats moored in False Creek and Coal Harbour. Robin still has pictures of sailboats all over his office and dreams of spending his retirement years cruising the Caribbean. When asked how easy it would be for a 65-year-old man and his (admittedly much younger) wife to handle a sailboat, he is evasive. Maybe he could hire some Cubans but what if they mutinied or tried to fuck his wife? He refuses to consider taking his wife's two strapping teenage boys, who are supposed to be with their father but are always around Robin's house. A couple of months ago, one of them had to be forcibly removed by the police.

In due course, the union convinced an arbitrator that Robin had been laid off unjustly. He could easily teach in Adult Preparatory Education, where new faculty had recently been hired. One of these new faculty was told to walk, and Robin was reinstated and his salary for his year of wandering paid up in full. He still had to sell his house to cut his losses, and even at that he owed the bank $20,000. However, the sailboat dream is still a possibility. With only ten years to go to full pension Robin, as he himself often wryly puts it, "has it made."

Kurt is a specialist in German influences on English romanticism. He teaches Canadian Literature. He is surrealistically German and his younger students are always asking me if maybe he could be a war criminal hiding out in Canada and maybe someone should turn him in. I point out that he would've been, at most, only 10 years old when the war ended. Still, they are suspicious. He's very popular with his older students, however, because he discusses all the great ideas in infinite detail and listens to their views even if he disagrees.

Kurt's financial problems started when he bought a lot on one of the Gulf Islands and then, receiving a small inheritance when his father died, started a house on it in preparation for early retirement. Because this house was conceived of mostly in this town, where winter lasts for six months, Kurt's dreams of the sea became mellow. For example, in addition to casements opening to the foam, sunny pleasure domes, etc., the house obviously had to have a boat launch and pier which, as it turned out, in that part of the island meant a breakwater, which was impossible. However, the people who contracted to build it never told Kurt that, and a lot of money was wasted trying to get gigantic boulders to sit on top of one another in the tide-torn water. Kurt was also never told, until the house was half finished, that there was little or no water available in that part of the island and that, consequently, fire insurance on such a large house would be astronomical. Suddenly he realized why everyone else in the area lived in a shack. He became very concerned about his collection of nineteenth-century German Romantic poetry being lost in a fire. He decided to have a fireproof bunker blasted for it out of the rock, away from the house but connected to it by a covered cedar walkway that wound over the rocks like a fuse. Security was also a problem, since Kurt and his family could only visit the island during the summer months. The house was constantly being vandalized.

Finally, Kurt ran out of money and credit and couldn't finish the house. It had no power, plumbing, heating or even windows. He rented it to some locals who paid less than a quarter of his monthly payments to live in it. These people stapled plastic over the windows, put in Coleman stoves and lights, installed stovepipes and an airtight heater, and moved in. For a few summers, Kurt and his family tented on the edge of the property, as far away as they could get from the faded, unfinished house, the piles of boards and broken bricks, and the old boats, broken plastic toys and rusted lawnmowers and baby carriages that filled up the dusty yard. Eventually, they decided to sell, but nobody would buy at any reasonable price. Finally, Kurt stopped going to the place and merely paid the bills. However, the original architect's drawings are still tacked to the office wall and Kurt can often be seen staring dreamily at them. Early retirement is now out of the question, and Kurt has recurring nightmares about the tenants burning his largely uninsured Valhalla to the ground. But in another fifteen years, barring layoff, cardiac arrest or social revolution, he will be there.

And what about me? Admittedly I'm not into boats or houses but how probable is it really that I will write a great novel and get to Hollywood and meet Jane Fonda? Will she be able to keep her body up that long? Or will I really go, say, to Guatemala (as Connie and Wally recommend) where they have shot pretty well all the peasants and indians in order to pay the interest on their debt and make the place safe for corporate capitalism and visiting gringos? I could live on $5 a day and wear a white suit and straw hat and sit in outdoor cafes and bars and write novels like Malcolm Lowry. How reasonable is my worship of Tom Wolfe in the practise of which I keep a copy of *The Purple Decade* on my office bookshelf beside all the rhetoric and technical style handbooks so that in moments of doubt and confusion I can stare yearningly at the picture of Tom on the dustcover? He is sitting at an outdoor cafe, alone, with a drink on the table, an umbrella over the arm of his chair, and a Mona Lisa smirk on his face as might befit a man who did, after all, in the guise of writing mere journalism, produce some of the century's greatest fiction. But do I have Tom's insight? Will I make it? Chances are, if I do, there will be a mug of Geritol rather than a drink on the table, a cane rather than an umbrella on the arm of my chair, and my smirk will be spoiled by loose dentures.

At least, with luck, I still have a few years to go. So does my dad, it seems. By Wednesday he was up and about. There was some talk of an operation on his prostate, which had caved in due to the heart attack, but that was in the future. Meanwhile, he had a plastic tube and a bag hooked to his leg. He wasn't worried about losing his prostate. He said it was time to forget about sex and concentrate on dying, which was turning out to be a full-time job.

Victoria and I left him and my mom in the non-smoking common room holding hands and watching TV. We drove to a Gastown cafe where I told her how proud I was of her and gave her some money so she could get her handbrake fixed, buy a set of tires, pay the rent and generally finish off the term in the manner to which she has become accustomed. She was depressed about her Grandpa so I entertained her with stories about my colleagues. She thought they were funny but more in the telling than in fact. I said they would be entirely funny if I could just learn how to tell them right.

I was back at work on Thursday morning. I found out that things weren't going so well for Barry. "My dad called last night," he said. "My mom's out of it. Most of the time she thinks she's in Los Angeles and he's down to see her. When he rolls her down the hall and shows her the Calgary landmarks, she figures he's arranged things to trick her. Gets quite pissed off at him. The doctors say she has brain damage."

I was sorry for Barry and his mom. I was glad it wasn't me. Soon it will be me, but soon even Tom Wolfe will be staring at a blank wall. Probably he always, in a way, has. How else did his mind's eye get so sharp? Dreams are ok if you keep them out of your daily life. Meanwhile, it if comes down to any real choices between this town and Hollywood, the ward nurse and Jane Fonda, the college or the farm, work or leave, I'll probably take the former. You can't write about nothing. You can't invent the truth.

Captive of the Klondike.

I should be reading the new editions of the short story and technical writing textbooks that have been foisted on my unsuspecting colleagues and self by the multinational publishers. But who are these assholes, mostly younger than me now, intruding their standard English into the dialogue of the gods? And who are these other assholes claiming that technicians are intent on speaking and writing, in plain words, the truth?

Tell that to some of my former students – the five-foot, 180-pound future lab tech, for example, whose favourite hobby seemed to be collecting discarded wristbands from the hospital parking lot during field trips, and his classroom buddy, the wizened and militantly proud AA member with the death-rattle cough who had spent over half his adult life "travelling." From the kitchen exhaust register behind the Blackstone Hotel down Granville to the liquor store, perhaps, but then no doubt through some (unspecifiable) miracle into the white light of permanent sobriety and five years at the pulp mill pulling asbestos off the pipes and walls until the asbestos was all gone (partly into his lungs) and thence, via Canada Manpower, into college, Technical Communication, Unit One: Resumés. Old Larry just nodded when I put a red line through all his activities at AA. A few minutes later, back at the computer, I heard him wheeze, "Fred, you don't have to put in your weight and height." "Won't they find out if I get an interview?" "That's where you charm them." For Fred's resumé, where the "Personal" section was the big problem, they finally agreed on "Health: Excellent" and, for a hobby, "Walking."

In the short story book, the forces of professionalism are subtler. Freshman English has a longer tradition than Technical Communication. Its professors, among whom I count myself when asked, have learned humility, a devious virtue. We have Shakespeare, Swift and Joyce to tell us that the twentieth century is a dark age, that modern ideas and accomplishments are largely the same old shit and that honesty, clarity, energy and all the other attributes of genius are not grist for the professional mill but grind the mill itself. We further know that our job is to throw ourselves into said mill, to lubricate, coat and isolate the essential irritant with our own blood, shit, sweat, tears and any other useful materials that can be rendered out of us (and new derivatives are always being discovered). Noble work when done honestly, and like any other work, something to do with dedication (rather then enthusiasm) and in fair expectation of material reward. So it is that the stories in this book are arranged alphabetically by author's name and with short and mainly biographical introductions. This is why we use this book. It has no thematic, stylistic or (despite the no doubt justifiable prominence of Northrop Frye) mythopoeic groups. It has no lists of secondary sources. It shows, in the professional sense, taste.

But of course the temptation to cut corners is irresistible when one is on the forced run, head down and ass up and snapping, to Saturday, payday, vacation and retirement. See Dick read a story. See Dick easily understand its socially redeeming merit. See Dick pass the course and become a dentist who will not tie Jane down into the chair and make her suck his cock. See the majority of parents, administrators, public officials, judges, leaders of special interest groups and politicians easily understand what Dick will understand and continue to pay and protect the teacher. And so it also is that, for example, the first story in the text, by Margaret Atwood, is written in third person, past tense (the iambic pentameter of prose), with the retrospective parts in (it is to laugh) past-perfect. There are similes for colour, and the theme, as the editor puts it, concerns the intrusion of middle-class Canadian values into the third world and the role of women in a male-dominated society. Gag me, as my students used to say, with a spoon. Bring on the dwarfs.

Were I famous enough to be included in this book, I would occur between Graham Greene and Mark Helprin. Greene was in the old edition, an old stand-by suspiciously to be counted on for setting, character, plot and theme, and yet conveniently blessed with an international reputation that transcends the textbooks and reaches, even, Hollywood. But does he express the ultimate theme of art, which is "Look at me, you boring assholes . . ."? I personally doubt it, but am willing to leave the question of Greene's genius to posterity, that useful bunch, to decide. The important point is that he is amenable to the clear delineation and measurement of established objectives. In other words, it is possible to produce multiple-choice tests based on his stories. Helprin, on the other hand, is unfamiliar, a new addition to the text. I frown on new additions, but understand that there must be at least the impression of progress. Helprin is, naturally, younger than me, a former member of the Israeli Airforce and British Army, one who has obviously "lived" and has, there-fore (as the lay person might naively but, also all too safely, assume), "something to say." I don't want to read his story. It's too early in the day, too late in the summer, for me to dis-cover genius and with it the implication that I'm a long long way down the road to nowhere.

Not that I am, entirely, a navel-gazing, ball-scratching, pen-pushing academic. Hell no. Connie has gotten me into hiking, travelling and eating fish. Just in time, too. One has one's heart to worry about, without which one can scarcely hope to fall in love, join the communists or collect a pension. In the pictures that Connie brought out last night, as a kind of peace offering, I look dashing enough in knee brace, sun visor, khaki shorts and Raichle hiking boots, silent upon a peak in Kluane. But of course, I don't overdo it. The life of adventure is not for me. I'm short-sighted. I've got a tricky prostate. I don't like monopolizing and spraying over public toilets. I wouldn't want to end up in the army or jail. As I understand it, they bumhole you if you have to get up in the middle of the night. Finally, I have a hyper imagination. It is easily enough deflected from its main work of getting me up in the morning, worrying about the kids and figuring out the pension plan.

This summer, for example, my imagination has been possessed by bears. As I marched along the hiking trail to the beat of an accelerated heart, my imagination encountered bears, fought them off with knife, gun and sword, rescued my kids, Connie and a number of vague, dishevelled, long-limbed women from them, and sweated through long nights in windy mountain passes convulsively devising and field-testing claw-proof aluminum-mesh sleeping bags, propane stove canisters that double as grenades or flame-throwers, and bear-repellent creams, lotions and vaginal jellies.

What a waste. I blame the Yukon Park Service. In the warden's office at Haines Junction, I came face to crotch with a standing, stuffed grizzly – fit usher to the delights of wilderness hiking in the icefields of Kluane Park and over the Chilkoot Pass on the historic "Trail of '98." While the warden was writing down our names, names and phone numbers of next-of-kin, and colours of tent and sleeping bags so that our camp (or the scattered remains thereof) could be spotted by air, I read the sign. *Ursus horribilis*, 1200 lbs, speeds up to 60 mph. His claws were the length of dinner knives. The warden noticed my concern. "They're mostly up in the alpines now," he said. "They browse on the new shoots that come up as the snow melts. Just don't take them by surprise." He pushed some pamphlets at me.

Connie led me outside. "As long as we make lots of noise

and don't eat or screw in the tent we're ok," she said. She was right. Except for some ambiguity as to whether you should keep your pack on (to protect your back) or drop it (as an offering) the instructions were clear. Burn all leftover food and food bags. Wash and pack out all tin cans and bottles. Keep sweaty hiking clothes and boots out of the tent at night. No sex, heterosexual in particular (though the bear will prefer the woman in this case). And finally, over and over, for those who might have a choice in the matter, DO NOT FEED.

I suppose the Park Service has good reason to have the grizzly on display. They've apparently lost two tourists since June, one in a campsite and one by a roadside garbage can. According to the pamphlets, more people are killed by bears on the side of the road than in the bush. Some people have lazy imaginations. For them, bears are childhood, the disappearing wilderness, past tense. They will walk up to bears and offer then hotdogs. They will send their kids over to pose for a photo. We heard of a family that drove their car up to a grizzly that was dipping into a garbage can. The father rolled his window down to take a snapshot and the little girl in the back seat showed her teddy to the grizzly. The grizzly proceeded to dismantle the car. Fortunately, some other tourists saw what was happening and pulled in and caused enough noise and confusion to drive the grizzly off. Goldilocks got away but her car was scattered all over the highway. Of course, only God or maybe Freud but probably not Northrop Frye knows what might've happened to her imagination while the roof and windows were caving in on her head.

But all this just goes to show why I am not in the textbook between Greene and Helprin. If they visited the Yukon, they would not be worried about present-tense bears. Faced with the colourful and contained history of the place, they would immediately fly there on the hopefully viewless wings of poesie and they or reasonable facsimiles thereof would fight off Soapy Smith and his gang in Skagway, where cruise ships now dock and helicopters piloted by embittered Vietnam vets whizz camera-laden tourists up to the pass and over to the glaciers to observe and, as the warden at Sheep Camp put it, scare shitless the bears. Or, laden with the mandatory half-ton of supplies and provisions, they would hike through the narrow strip of coastal forest, following the glacial rivers upward, confronting the capitalist trolls who built the makeshift bridges and skylines and charged exorbitant prices to the hurried miners. They would stop in the cafes, saloons and whorehouses of Canyon City and Sheep Camp before finally picking their way over the rocking boulders of the pass and across the permanently snowy crest where Alaska ends and Canada starts. There they would be checked by the Men in Scarlet for the prescribed supplies and told not to drink, gamble, fight, light fires without a permit or shoot indians on sight. Then, wondering no doubt if such picky regulations, well-meaning though they may be, don't unnecessarily infringe on personal freedom and thus have a debilitating effect on the human spirit, and keeping their guns loaded just in case, they would struggle through the alpines and down into Bennett Lake and thus by boat or dog-team down the Yukon River system 300 more miles to Dawson City where they would see strange sights by the northern lights.

My closest brush with history came in the porta-john at Sheep Camp. When hiking, I am always attracted to these disinfected and well-stocked fibreglass incubators, these outriders of civilization, even though they would provide little protection against a bear if it came to that. I imagine that, were I mauled to death on the trail, the general opinion would be that I was an asshole anyway for being there. However, if I got killed in a porta-john with my pants around my ankles there would be outrage. Public property and human dignity are sacred. There would be calls for tougher johns, more wardens and a general clean-up of delinquent bears and I might even get a campsite named after me. In this particular john the warden, who was at the time hunched over the campfire with Connie and a coffee swapping stories about Central America where he'd spent eight years as a "missionary," had thoughtfully placed a hardcover edition of Pierre Berton's *I*

Remember Klondike. This book (some pages missing) was a retired veteran of the "Library of the Alaska Parks Service." I looked up Sheep Camp and was amazed to learn that I was shitting virtually in the middle of a tent city that stretched for a half-mile up the creek. I was also amazed at the stories of the partying and fighting that went on. For the miners, this was the last stop stateside and the last touch of a marine climate. After Sheep Camp they lined up (like sheep) to ascend the pass and face the mounties and permanent winter. It occurred to me that one of Berton's research assistants (prime examples all, rumour has it, of Canadian nubility) had no doubt hiked this trail taking notes for the book and perhaps had even settled her firm and rosy posterior comfortably into the same hole that my infirm, grey and slightly shrunken one now plugged. Maybe she too felt safe in porta-johns, and had here written the first draft of the very pages I was reading.

I admit that it's a great story. A human tide washed into the Yukon and out again, leaving the country littered with government-protected and often embarrassingly personal artifacts – boot soles, bean tins, stove lids, belts, hats, gloves and medicine and whisky bottles. The miners in the laminated photos (set into aluminum frames and bolted to concrete at all pertinent locations along the trail) look mainly bored but resigned, not unlike my students on registration day. One can imagine the jokes, philosophizing, embarrassment, sense of déjà vu, stories and stupidity. But history repeats itself, roughly, every half hour, so why settle for long-ago half hours when the present one is breathing in your face, inescapable, interminable? What point can be made, quickly and with colour and vehemence, in past tense? Ultimately, it's all deniable, the witnesses dead, forgotten, discredited or discreditable.

So, pumped up by fresh air and bronzed by the sun, I was glad to finally get away from history and bears, to arrive at Bennett Lake where our faithful indian charterboat captain was waiting at the campsite with root beers, to feel the powerful outboard carry us up the huge and sparkling lake while we stretched our tired leg and shoulder muscles in the sun, to arrive at a Whitehorse cafe and ingest a greasy burger with fries and to crawl into a safe bed around Connie at my brother's house. I was glad too, the next morning, to find a card waiting for me from my son with the cryptic but all-too-well understood message (he being a man of few and carefully-chosen words), "I got laid-off at the garage. Bruce helped me fix the truck. I hope you are safe and still have your wallet. Love, Wesley."

Connie didn't share my enthusiasm for either the end of our vacation or the card from Wes. She is convinced that someday something in me will snap and I will hit the trail with her forever. Or we will visit Guatemala which, at $10 per day for meals, hotels and booze, is Connie's idea of paradise. She figures it will be my idea too when I realize that I could retire early there on the lousy $30,000 that, sorted, dried, weighed and packaged, I am presently worth. She sees me in straw hat, white suit and sandals, sitting in a sidewalk cafe with a cup of powerful Guatemalan coffee and a dense manuscript (or is it dense coffee and a powerful manuscript?) while she and some other adventuresome geriatrics head for the Darien gap, with bags of Canadian maple-leaf pins in their packs and $50 (U.S.) stitched into the linings of their hiking pants.

She is also convinced that my abilities as a father are roughly equivalent to those I exhibit as a teacher – viz, negligible. The truck has long been a case in point: that Wes is working and spending his money on it instead of studying for higher grades, that I encourage him in this and even contribute some of the money that I'm supposed to be saving for travel, unpaid leave and retirement, and that I tend to buy Wes's way out of tough situations, thus contributing to the upbringing of a wimp who will never become a dentist and support his old dad. Connie never made such mistakes with her daughters. It was sink or swim for them, and they bobbed.

But what do women know about the subtleties of father-son bonding? I too, as a youth, dreamed of such things as racing pistons, ported manifolds and twin-barrel carbs. But I only dreamed; my son actually touches these things. Last summer we rebuilt the old horse-barn into a shop, wired it and purchased a generator and electric drill. Then we dragged in a couple of rusting Datsun pickups from the back forty and proceeded to rebuild one. It took us a year to mix and match until we had a promising truck. This summer, Wes rebuilt the motor from the oil pan up. His plans were to finish the truck and then drive it down to his mother's in Victoria, arriving just in time to help his mother move into her newly-purchased house. Then he would return home for school. It was a vision of adolescent achievement that had my deepest sympathy. The deal was I would get back from the Yukon, test-drive the truck and, if it proved road-worthy, stand him to the insurance and he would pay me back later when he got another part-time job. Of course, the merely financial details were vague and, until yesterday, entirely hidden from Connie.

On Friday afternoon, when Connie and I arrived home, I discovered that Wes had hidden a few details from me. The truck was running alright, but while I stood there admiring the gleaming engine and its throaty roar, the bucket seats imported from the 1968 Maverick behind the hay shed, the sportscar dash picked up at the wrecking yard for a mere $150 and the $200 stereo, I couldn't help noticing at the same time the absence of a handbrake, a feature held in absolute contempt by Wes and Bruce and removed to make room for the dash and stereo. I also noted the absence of tailpipe, hood (to make room for the carbs), seat belts and tires with treads. I noticed hardened and cracked heater and hydraulic brake hoses, the same old rusted, dented and in places suspiciously damp brake lines and the windshield split clear across in three places.

I test-drove it yesterday, while Connie was in town buying some outfits for work. We took it out onto the stretch of dirt logging road that runs from our farmyard gate 300 miles to the Rockies. I didn't have to go that far, though it appeared that the truck might actually have been able to make it. I drove twenty miles, stomping the brakes, swerving, putting the accelerator to the floor. Nothing went wrong, except for a minor heater hose leak into the cab on the passenger side. The truck ran, as Wes said it would, like snot. I finally pulled over by a blue lake and sat down at the forest-service picnic table to let the roar of the truck seep out of my ears. When Wes pulled in beside me in my truck, we had it out.

First, I complimented him on the engine job. Then, I told him he wouldn't get halfway to Victoria without being pulled over. The noise and the missing hood would attract attention and the missing handbrake and cracked windshield would ground him for good. He said he'd chance it. It was the old stand-off. Would I break first and refuse to allow him to do what I'd more or less agreed to, under conditions that he'd more or less met? Or would he break first and apply what he referred to as "the old quivering lip treatment" that invariably led to victory but at great cost to his adolescent self-esteem?

I speculated that the truck would be useful around the farm for hauling wood and gravel. Surprisingly, Wes agreed. I offered $500. He'd put $700 into it. I wondered if I needed a $200 stereo to haul wood. But I kept my mouth shut. When he gets back from Victoria I can always get him to gut out the stereo and install it in the upstairs room. I looked out across the lake. The insurance, if I bought it for him, would be almost $400, and there would be small chance of getting it back. If he broke down en route and got picked up, the financial implications could be serious. If he had an accident ... but I didn't want to think about that.

"Sold," I said.

When we got back, Connie was making coffee. Before I could stop him, Wes told her that he'd sold the truck to me. When he saw the blank look of disbelief on her face, he lied coolly and massively about the price.

I was impressed. He's a man, I thought. Connie walked out, got into her car and left.

Later, after I paid Wes the first installment on the truck, I dropped him off at his sister's place for the night. I decided that I needed a drink. I found Barry and Meryl at the usual table. Meryl is one of Barry's creative writing students from the good old days when the college thought it had a cultural mandate. He has published one book of poems and works for a society for the mentally challenged, conducting outings for them to the pulp mills, police station, and college, and arranging job opportunities for those who can dish up soup without opening their mouths. He is good with the mentally challenged because he can relate to them, in detail, every episode of the *Gilligan's Island* and *Mr. Ed* reruns that he watched when he was in public school. "They don't make shows like that any more," he complains. He pulled an expensively nondescript Vancouver college creative writing magazine out of his back pocket. They'd printed a collection of his poems and referred to him in the biographical blurb in the back as "Ms."

"It could be an advantage," said Barry. "The lesbians are putting out some of the best magazines in the country right now."

"What if they want to meet me?" asked Meryl.

They both figured I made a good move in buying the truck. "What else could you do?" said Barry. "He'd kill himself in it. You'll probably kill yourself in it. He'll be on the bus tomorrow and you'll be able to sleep. Anyway, he would've got the $300 off you one way or the other."

I shifted uncomfortably. Of course I'd censored out the real price. I didn't want to look like a complete rube. The waitress came by with another round and we all stared mutely at her bared, Amazonian shoulders. Maybe single life would be ok after all.

"You have to write fuck poetry to get into those magazines," said Meryl glumly. "I can't do that. No experience, though I suppose in some schools that could be considered an advantage."

"I never had any luck with lesbian editors," I said.

"That reminds me," said Barry. "I took your book to Toronto in July. My publishers love it. They want to publish it next spring."

This was nothing new. My stories have been kicking around the edges of the Canadian literary world for some time now. My friends are always trying to get them published for me. In the immediately previous attempt, my friend Stan showed them to his left-wing publisher in Vancouver. However, some people on the editorial collective thought the stories were sexist. In May I left Wes at Connie's and went down and Stan and I talked it over in a bar where they were showing a porno video about two guys delivering pizzas to a Sons of Norway lodge. Stan bought the beer, apologized for keeping the book for so long and swore that if the left couldn't get its sexual shit together soon he was going to give it all up and join a monastery.

I was mildly disappointed. The idea of being associated with the left wing and maybe blacklisted out of the U.S. or (more usefully) Guatemala, sounded very romantic. However, I can never get very excited about publication. I used to dream about it but now, in the sixteenth year of my seniority and the sixth of my pension plan, it seems beside the point and something that could even be a nuisance. On the other hand, I'm not against it. As Barry says, it does get the stuff off your desk so you can stop fussing with it. He also points out that his publishers are very witty, sensitive, intelligent people with nice houses in Toronto. You can get readings and stay over. You can exchange letters with them and make contacts with the other writers they publish, some of whom are, Barry seems to believe, beautiful, mature, heterosexual women who like men.

You can also, if you publish a book, get in line for government grants. Of course these grants are small, but for steadily-employed people like Barry and me they can mean the difference between an old Underwood and a lap computer, of Xmas in New York instead of Vancouver. Mainly, though, they provide a foundation on which tax deductions can be built. If you earn money as a writer, you can claim as a writer. Of course if you only earn as a writer, you are starving and tax deductions are not relevant. But if you have a steady

- 142 -

job, as Barry and I emphatically if thanklessly do, these deductions can be significant.

You could, for example, on the strength of yearly royalties on a modest book of poems amounting to, say, $100, claim 10 percent of all your telephone, gas, rent, entertainment, mail, travel, electricity and babysitting bills as writing expenses. These expenses are deducted from your total salary each year and the tax you pay is considerably reduced. Instead of paying out $50, you might get $5000 back. Rumours are that a writer, employed at a university (or perhaps I should say, a professor who writes) can save enough on income tax each year to make the mortgage payments on a house or spend four months touring Europe.

The trick is to keep your earnings as a writer as low as possible, and your activities and deductions as high as possible, without making the tax people suspicious. For most writers, the first two requirements are easy. It is the third that causes trouble.

Barry, for example, doesn't use his tax deductions. His muse has, as he says, hard tits. He can't produce a book in ten years, let alone one. He has trouble convincing some of his best friends that he's a poet. Anyway, he knows writers who have gone into deductions and the strain is terrific. Low production and sales could be a sign of low talent. On the other hand, they could be a sign of genius. The accountants tend to accept the first assumption since they are into numbers, while artists tend to accept the second as a matter of self-defence. In their attempts to convince the tax people of their genius, some poets have published their freshman class notes and their mother's diaries. Dramatic monologues based on the histories of famous people are big; you get more bulk for less introspection. Some poets even get into children's literature, science fiction and versions of classic poems in translation. If they go to the dentist, they write about it. One poet had a mental breakdown because he was being investigated by the Revenue Department. He wrote a series of poems about it. The poems were pretty good, for a change, probably because the shit was running down his leg while he was writing them. The poems were published and the critics were impressed and the book sold enough to get the poet off the hook for another year.

Sometimes Barry gets very angry about all of this. It does mean, after all, that massive amounts of shit have to be foisted on an already impatient or indifferent public. Last night, however, he was philosophical. Probably it was the beer, but also he was just back from two weeks in New York visiting the jazz bars and hanging around William Carlos Williams' house. This always tends to cheer him up unless he suddenly remembers his Chargex in which case he starts to rave about people with university jobs who can go to work irregularly and even drunk and get four months off in the summer for research, which usually amounts to re-hashing the critical perspective on some dead expatriate Brit who couldn't write in the first place.

"I've heard some scary stories," he said. "Apparently you can write off your library. A library is supposed to be essential if you're a writer, though I prefer beer or even videos. One guy decided to mention the names of some musicians in his poems so he could write off his stereo and records. It sounds reasonable to me but he got nailed. Another trick is to donate your rough copies to a library. The library agrees to appraise your donation at a price they would never dream of paying for it and then you deduct this sum off your wages as a gift to charity."

Barry does make extra money by doing odd jobs for the Canada Council. This enables him to buy his kids some of the little extras like trail bikes, lap computers and bedroom TV sets. He sits on juries to decide who gets grants. He says it's like reading freshman papers. You mark them out of ten. You get a wage and three trips a year to places where the jury meets to make decisions. One catch is you have to read a lot of pompous begging letters. "Most of these fuckers," says Barry, "quit work years ago to dedicate themselves to their art. Now they think they deserve pensions." Another catch is that you have to go to information meetings at these various places and mingle with the local artists. He says the ones on the Island are the worst. He says they are all remittance-men Brits who write novels about their youths in the Welsh countryside where they learned to fuck sheep, or lesbian poets who want to be witches or mermaids and kill men. They all listen to CBC and complain about being neglected. Once, in Tofino, he was asked how he presumed he could possibly judge the needs of Island artists. "Easy," he said. "Most of you need to be bumfucked with a hot poker." The Council officials suggested that he go for a long walk by the ocean.

Barry figures that I shouldn't get involved in any of this. "You've got a job," he says. "Enough is enough." However, I figure I could handle it. I'm 45. I could use a bit more variety in my working life. Also, I've learned to manage money. Every night when I tuck into bed I review my savings and investments. In one account I save for Wes's university education in case he ever wants one. In another I save in case Victoria burns out at the hospital and needs a trip to Hawaii or Jen gets sick of working in the computer store and decides to become a lawyer or accountant. I dream of them all brilliant and successful, driving sporty Japanese cars and flying to New York for first nights. "A gift from dad," they would say to their admiring friends. I buy bonds and the maximum in retirement plans every year. I read the economic news that looks bad for the young but good for mature types like me with steady jobs and seniority. My kids aren't going to suffer if I can help it. Frankly, I plan to hang onto my job until they chop my fingers off. I figure that, as a writer, I could get a few grants and deductions and credits that will make it easier for me to hang on and harder for them to chop.

Helprin's story, thank God, turns out to be a facile allegory of no significance except that it echoes Coleridge's "Rhyme of the Ancient Mariner," Poe's "Narrative of Arthur Gordon Pym," and Conrad's "Secret Sharer." In other words, it provides the instructor with the opportunity to deliver lectures that draw upon his or her childhood experience, divorce, philosophy of life and knowledge of English and American literature, and to design open-ended exam questions that would require students to know everything about life and literature and thus permit the instructor to pass or fail them on the truly relevant grounds of whether or not they throw spit balls in class. Such stories can be invaluable, though it's best if they are covered at the end of semester. The students get confused, however, if I don't do the stories in order of appearance in the textbook. Students tend to read in the time they have between classes, if they read at all (though I cover for this by the random administration of multiple-choice tests). Helprin, if I teach him, will have to come after Greene, or there will be chaos.

I'll probably teach him. When I dropped Barry off last night, he said he'd picked out a few new stories that had potential. We arranged to get together tomorrow to sort things out, though probably we'll go to the bar instead and end up watching the snake dancer and her audience. Classes are not for another week and we tend to savour the last days of relative freedom right down to the last minute. Anyway, it's surprising how many great multiple-choice questions, not to mention other major professional and personal decisions, can come to you while you are watching a stripper coaxing the head or tail of a comatose boa constrictor towards various parts of her anatomy.

When I got home I found Connie waiting for me with a bottle of wine and the photos. She apologized for trying to run my life even though she still thinks I'm fucking up, and agreed to come to dinner and see Wes off. We kissed and made up. We took the wine to bed.

Local Initiatives.

I'm in the Sears cafeteria, drinking coffee and writing. I just did the grocery shopping. Wesley and his class are on a field trip to the skating rink. He is having a change.

I bought a book in the meat department. They have a sale bin there. It's a biography of Dorothy L. Sayers. I had a look at it while my coffee was cooling. Dorothy was an energetic lady all her life. A chainsmoker. She was quietly eccentric and religious and did church work. Never a dull moment. She got fatter and fatter and finally she had a heart attack. She was in the middle of her translation of the *Paradiso*. She was at the bottom of the stairs. Her body couldn't take the weight of her accomplishments.

My accomplishments evaporate like gasoline. For the fifteenth year in a row I scored "mildly interesting" in my teaching evaluations. Ten percent of my students thought I was "very good." Ten percent thought I was a jerk. This seems reasonable to me. However, compared to forty thousand instructors across the continent, I'm in the bottom ten percentile. Maybe English is not a popular course. Maybe the Americans are better teachers. Maybe the computer fucked up. The managers are upset. The union is investigating.

Meanwhile, I teach for fifteen hours a week, sit in the office for five but nobody comes. I carry my writing and marking in a shoulder bag. I do five papers in the Chuckwagon at Pine World, five in the Simon Fraser Hotel coffee shop, a few more at home. When I run out of papers, I work on a story.

It's important to have things to do and places to go. Sears is good because it is big and varied. In the north, this is crucial. You can spend a couple of hours here, maybe three if you have lunch. Right now it is thirty below outside. Snow is blowing in from Dawson Creek, piling up. The city has run through its budget for clearing snow and trucking it out onto river ice. No one knows if the city will keep trucking or not. Meanwhile, the garden tractors are lined up in the mall, waiting for spring. The mannequins are wearing bikinis.

There is a problem with heavy boots and coats. If I were a businessman, I would cater to this. You could make a fortune checking boots and galoshes. Better, you could rent conveyances so people could push their coats, boots, kids and purchases around. People don't like things taken away from them. The heating system could break down. There could be a fire. The Russians could come thundering over the North Pole, spreading death and communism.

The bush is always there, around the edges of everyone's eyes, empty, a promise. Once it covered this town thick and silent. It was pushed back to make room, converted into heat, canoes, forts, buildings, roads. In Sears, there are pictures that document this process, scenes from the town's historical past. They are a testimony to progress. The fort is built, the indians are offered better land somewhere, anywhere, the tents give way to wood frame buildings, the railway comes and takes the men to war, the old wooden buildings burn down and are replaced by brick. The eye seeks out the bush, fringing the cutbanks, in the sloughs along the river, carpeting the sleeping hills to the north.

The Russians plan everything first, in five-year increments, and then they do it. Winter and space congeal them. They believe in mind over materialism. This is what makes them so dangerous. They start with essentials – fur coats and vodka. The fur is genuine and the vodka is ninety-eight proof and they virtually give them away. Everyone gets a couple pounds of meat every week and lots of cheap Black Sea oil. Their only danger is falling asleep outside and freezing to death. Russian streets are long and empty. Everything is locked up at five o'clock. Boredom is a significant factor. No amount of planning will solve this problem.

We believe it is more natural to take things as they come. Planning is hard work. There are obvious similarities between Simon Fraser's fort and Spruce Centre Mall where Sears is. You can see similarities between Simon Fraser, whose portrait hangs over the salad bar, and the latest manager who is close to the cash register. There are further pictures with captions like "Fraser Prepares to Explore the River that Bears His Name" and "Danger!" The first shows the Fort, a palisade enclosing three log cabins. A field of stumps separates the Fort from the bush. In the foreground, men are knee-deep in the river loading two canoes. The second picture shows a man in buckskin holding onto an overturned canoe as it slips into the rapids. You assume that this is not Simon Fraser.

Nowadays, there isn't much danger in working for the Bay, except maybe unemployment. They have a store in the downtown area. It is as big as Sears and has a nice cafeteria in the basement but the suburbs are moving further and further out and the people with money don't come downtown to shop. City Council made a deal with the Bay for a big complex in the downtown area. They put up six square blocks of property that they agreed to buy, mostly from themselves. They circulated pictures of cities with rotten cores. They devised a plan for a development that would bring Eaton's in and introduce over a million square feet of retail space into the downtown. There was a model in city hall with free coffee.

People weren't impressed. Sears and Woodward's fought back with their own expansion plans and free coffee. They argued that free enterprise was at stake. Let the city council plan sewers, they said. When the elections came, most of city council went down. I wasn't sorry. The old town has a certain charm. It is not all locked up at night. The wooden hotels have strippers and rock bands from Richmond, White Rock and Seattle. The chinese cafes stay open for as long as you can nurse a coffee. There are second-hand stores, basement karate dojos, billiard parlours and local art shops. Of course there are a lot of fires. There are also a lot of drunks around, scavenging beer and pop bottles, fighting, asking for handouts, and freezing to death in doorways on winter nights.

I miss the past. The bush has a tendency to seed itself in my head, take root and grow. In Sears I always sit under a picture of the town taken sometime in the Thirties, halfway between "Danger!" and a colour photo of Spruce Centre. I feel more at home here. In this picture the bush is still in view. You can imagine it turning red in spring. There are no paved streets and plenty of empty lots growing wild roses, indian paint brush, mint, camomile, buttercups and lupin. You can see the cutbanks clearly. The buildings are one or two storeys except the hotel which is three. Where city hall is now there is a small triangular-shaped park with a war memorial. The picture is bloated and grainy, but I can see a lady by the hotel on the wooden sidewalk. The sidewalk is elevated and runs in a circle for ten blocks through the central downtown area.

She could go into the Bay, Ray's Ford, Manning's Men's Wear, Rosie's Ice Cream, the Dandy-Pole Barber Shop, the Ritz Cafe, Interior Hardware, Ming's Cafe, T. Cake and Son Bakery, the Windsor Hotel, Smith Billiard, and many others. Someday I should do some research on this in the new library, write a book. I've never been in the library, but it's got skylights, underground parking, and a wrap-around patio with planters. It was a victory for the forces of liberalism and professionalism. It is the second stage in the plans for a culture centre that will incorporate the swimming pool (stage one) and a theatre and new arena. Due to budget constraints, the theatre and arena have been scrapped, so there's lots of gravel around and no one has to park underground.

I'd rather work for Ray or T. Cake than Simon Fraser. I'm not the adventurous type. I'd rather work for Sears than Ray, though the muzak here is enough to drive you to the truck stop. I like institutions. If I ever lose my job teaching I'll go into nursing and get a job in the hospital. I've done Cardio-Resuscitation and St. John's Ambulance, all paid for by the college. Maybe they're worried about my students passing out in class and hitting their heads on their desks. Maybe I'll do Industrial First-Aid this summer, just to keep my hand in. If I can't make it as a nurse I could work in a mill, sit all day in an office on a bale of band-aids and read novels.

My ex-wife worked in the hospital years ago, before she left town, and I used to go there and pick her up. I felt at home. There were lots of places to go and sit, chairs by the windows where the hallways end, roll-away room partitions parked in the halls, forgotten coffee urns, stacks of old *Time* magazines, underground tunnels where the change rooms, cafeteria, laundry and furnace rooms are.

The people in the hospital look interesting. I'm forty-five, wonder about getting old, am bored by the future. I like the kids at school but have trouble identifying. Patients may be rich or poor, young or old, male or female, famous or infamous: it's all mostly fiction. They are struggling with their bodies and improvements get less and less likely. The hospital keeps their valuables in a safe. Their names are written in chalk above their beds. Some are in their last room, going down their last hall, through their last door. The cemetery is out west, on the bank high over the winding river, facing south into the weather.

My ex-wife worked in the "Sunset Lodge" addition. She liked it. Colourful surroundings. Flowers everywhere. The girls who ran the ward were a real team. Never say die. They had lots of parties. They hit the bar regularly. In the last year my ex-wife worked there they entered the Mardi Gras sno-golf contest. They decorated a snowmobile like an ambulance and put on crash helmets with red crosses and smacked purple tennis balls around the golf course. They took first prize. They got their pictures in the paper and brought in lots of cash for macramé on the ward. The next day the snow started to melt. It was an early thaw. It was a miracle. The disc jockeys from the local stations were phoning at 6 and 8 AM. They got free tickets to Reno and judged a male stripper contest.

Never say die. I meet some of them around town and they are still at it. They ask me how my ex-wife is doing in the south. Some of them have been working there for twenty years now. I'm cracking after fifteen. Actually, in the past couple of years I've done sweet fuck all. I'm losing my nerve. The lesson plans I give to the Dean are a mess. My outcomes don't match up with my objectives. Nothing is typed. Last year I didn't even cover the three novels on the list – *Johnny Got His Gun, To Kill a Mockingbird* and the requisite Canadian piece of Fenimore Cooper bullshit about Louis Riel. I hate it when white people write about indians. I gave them Conrad instead. Mostly, I talked about myself.

Last week I started shouting at the Principal. He says that the bottom ten percentile is no good. He has to account to the public. He wants me to write a report. I told him that was his job. Do your fucking job I told him. That was a mistake. If I got fired, funds would be low. There would be no music lessons and no dental care. No talent and no beauty. There would be no university education. No class and no money. Of course I would get six months severance pay to find a new life. Six months to get famous, finish up my novel and some articles. Wes and I could stretch it, move back to the farm, eat the bark off trees.

When I finish my coffee I have to go and pick Wes up and take him to the dentist for a cleaning. Then he is supposed to play his trumpet with the junior orchestra. He's worried about his mouth. Everybody's going to listen to him. Connie will come and my brother and his wife, and Peter who is her oldest kid by a previous marriage and one of my best friends. He is in town for a few days, buying supplies. Maybe we'll have a coffee after and Wes will go to bed with his head full of praise and his teeth aching.

All my kids play instruments. This makes me proud, as I have no musical talent myself. I try to follow along in Book One Toronto Conservatory with Mozart and Shostakovich.

Sometimes I fantasize that I'm playing the piano at the bar in the Vacation Inn. The Inn has only been around for a few years but already is on the skids. It's a good place to go if you want it quiet. It was going to be hooked up to the Bay development and provide convention facilities, shops, three movies, two cafes and a lounge. One cafe is shut down and the other has been taken over by a pancake franchise. The movies are doing ok but the shops are all empty, brown paper over the windows. They keep the building open because of the coal mines in the north. Someday, they say, the price of coal will go up and the local economy will boom and the place will be crawling with Japanese businessmen and bureaucrats from the south.

In my fantasy I have a tequila sitting on a napkin at the end of the keyboard and I have a little box with slips of paper for requests. A big party comes in and the hostess tells me that some guy named Don has just been promoted to Assistant Manager at Saveco. He likes Tony Bennett. I make a speech telling about Don and his promotion and I give a toast that gets rid of the third tequila for the night. I do "I Left My Heart in San Francisco." I wonder what it would be like to work for Don.

Peter plays piano and sometimes he works the bars when the bush closes for the summer. Seven years ago he was my student. I don't know what happened to him in high school but his writing was terrible. His essays were on pieces of paper that he pulled out of his pocket in crumpled balls and flattened out on my desk. I knew he was smart but I couldn't prove it. I couldn't read his work. One day I made him sit in my office and print his essay out on clean paper, double-spaced. This is part of my job and I wish I could get famous and quit. The school is considering diagnostic testing and more remedial courses with self-instructional modules on grammar, spelling and logic. This would certainly eliminate Peter and his problems. I went over his essay. There were brilliant flashes of insight but it still didn't make sense. He admitted it was crap. He admitted that he didn't know a complete sentence from Adam. I said nobody does but you learn to pretend. It's like a chord, I told him. You just hear it. He said he could hear chords easy but not sentences. He said he wanted to be a poet. I gave him a "B" and told him not to take any more English courses.

He quit college and moved to McBride, out in the country with all the middle-aged hippies who in the mid-Sixties sold their soybean cafes in Berkeley and bought Canadian land. His closest neighbour is a burnt-out rocker who repairs pianos, organs, nickleodeons and pinball machines, eats a pound of granola in the morning and goes like a camel all day. I admire this. In the country you can really feel at home, but it takes a lot of time and effort. If you know what colour of dirt you need for a garden, if you can read the wars of trees in their green circles of light, if you can think like an animal, then you have finally found yourself. You can go out gradually to where the dirt roads end and the trails start and the abandoned trapper's cabins sit on their quiet lakes. In the city, humility gets you nowhere. You have to invent you own work, turn the sun off and on, love like a sniper and work like a machine.

I've got literary projects coming out of my ass. A journal back east wants an issue on northern prose and a chapter for their literary history of Canada. Another wants reviews. I want stories. Maybe I'll get famous but it isn't easy. I've got problems. The Principal wants me to work on my lessons. I can't sit at a desk anymore. I write at the kitchen table and in laundromats. Long ago I loved libraries but I gave that up. Mainly, I work in cafes. I'm drinking too much coffee. I'm wired all the time. How can I write an article if I can't stay in the library? How can I write a novel when I'm always on the move?

On weekends when I'm on the farm I do a lot of hiking. I go into the bush as far as I can go. I put a couple of granola bars in my pocket. There are logging roads everywhere. You never see any animals. You can walk in safety, day and night. They know where you are. They have their own trails, beaten paths in snow or worn in clay, marked on the exposed roots of trees.

Hollows in the snow under pine, burrows, landmarks, tools of our trade. They cross our trails only occasionally and with great care. I can tell tracks of coyote, moose, rabbit, wolf, bear. If you walk far enough you come to a mill site. First there's cellar holes, bleached planks, car bodies in the willows. Then there's the sawdust heap, turned into black humus, the foundations of a mill and planer, cedar piles driven into the gravel down below the frost line. The whole country was cleared but you'd hardly think of that now, twenty or more years later. The pine and spruce are thick and pungent. In another hundred years, maybe, the loggers will be back, mills and towns going up.

Last autumn I met the president of the snowmobile club out there. He was on his Honda checking the trails, a Swede saw tied onto the back fender. He told me that his club leases two hundred square miles of land off the government for a dollar a year. Wilderness is cheap. I wondered if I was supposed to be there. He gave me a shot of rye. "You come a long way, walking," he said.

Somehow, I cleared the time for myself, pushed the people out. Can't seem to focus on much except a few stories that soak up all ambition except to leave things as they are. My ex-wife and the kids and I face our separate lives, duties to one another sliding away. The kids have learned how to go up and down hallways and respond to buzzers and bells. Down in Victoria my ex-wife takes her vaseline from room to room, rolling the patients over and soothing bed sores, massaging muscles, checking charts, talking. I push carts up and down the shopping centre aisles, fill the fridge, walk to work and back, mark papers. I walk to work in the early morning along silent streets, snow swept in winter, fragrant in summer. I walk back at night. Connie and I hit the bars and lounges downtown, have a cafe lunch on days off. I take my shoulder bag of papers and books off to the cafes.

This is my third refill. The lady who clears tables is starting to wonder. If I leave I'm ok; the day is sorted out. I wish the story was sorted out. Dorothy Sayers always had a project and a plan. Her list of works is impressive. She knew how things went. She ignored her fat. She puffed her cigarette. These are minor concerns. Of course they can kill you but that is always in the future. Meanwhile you can work. I wish I was that organized. I don't have a plan. I don't smoke or gain weight. If I did, I'd have something to write about. But if I get another coffee, I'll be happy for another hour. I'll think of something. Somebody will come in, say something.

About the author

John Harris was raised in Vancouver and White Rock, B.C., took degrees in English from the University of British Columbia and McGill, and has spent most of his adult life teaching English at the College of New Caledonia in Prince George, B.C.

For a free catalogue of all New Star titles, write to:
New Star Books Ltd.
2504 York Avenue
Vancouver, B.C.
V6K 1E3
tel. (604) 738-9429